101 HORROR
BOOKS TO READ
BEFORE YOU'RE
MURDERED

Sadie "Mother Horror" Hartmann

Co-owner of Night Worms and Editor-in-Chief of Dark Hart

FOREWORD BY **Josh Malerman**

ILLUSTRATIONS BY **Marco Fontanili**

PAGE STREET
PUBLISHING CO.

Dedicated to my mom and Stephen King

CONTENTS

Foreword by Josh Malerman

At risk of stepping on stage with too much flair, a note:

About halfway through this book, the book you now hold, I felt a few tears coming on. It was a justifiably unexpected turn; this being a book about horror novels, after all, not a sojourn into sap. That said, where have I cried more than I have within the pages of horror novels, where, as Sadie so perfectly describes it, coming-of-age is as powerful as body horror, as powerful as possession, too? But this isn't what overcame me. What climbed up inside had less to do with innocence conquering leviathan evil and much more to do with a specific individual's *accomplishment,* i.e. I thought: Can you believe what Sadie Hartmann *did* here?

Now, any nonfiction book must be only the tip of the iceberg, all research unseen. But when that book is an overflowing bibliography of an entire genre, said research includes hundreds, if not thousands, of books. To then whittle that down takes more than work. That takes heart.

So, forgive me for getting a little teary when I realized I was witnessing someone reaching their potential, touching greatness—that I was seeing a friend do exactly what she was born to do.

Sometimes I think us readers don't quite grasp how rare we are. To read a book a month is no less a feat than to read a dozen in the same four weeks. It's the *reading* that places you, me, us in the same circle, the same scene. And the horror reader is a unique animal. We recognize this in the eyes of our fellow junkies. There's a dark sparkle ever-present, and it never shines as black as it does when two of us cross paths. Therein lies the real beauty of this book: if you're well-versed in the modern macabre, you'll find yourself rooting for the names herein. And if you're new to all this? Oh man. Welcome. And Sadie's book *says* welcome. There are no snobs here. No know-it-alls. And definitely no walls.

Welcome to modern horror.

It's a vibrant place, with as much elasticity as the human mind can bend. From the tight bullet-thriller to bonkers absurdism, all is represented in these pages with the same respectful eye of the art lover stepping slowly through a museum of dark paintings. That someone is Sadie Hartmann, of course, who has had a knack for connecting people to books since the first post she ever made, the first book she ever recommended, the first time she must've felt a tapping on her shoulder, the fingertip of a well-meaning spirit who then whispered to her: *this can be what you do; this is what you will do.*

The voluminous asides mention many books that are not necessarily on the list of 101. Sadie's way of reminding us the genre is infinite for those willing to speak with it. And if it's all a bit overwhelming? Well, good. Sometimes being overwhelmed is the tell-tale sign of a relationship beginning. Note: The intentional omission of older classics was a telling move: what Sadie's saying is, modern books can and *will* become classics of their own. The books we're writing and reading right now. How thrilling is *that*?

So come on in, get loose, get into it. Each section of the book seduces in this way. Each category beguiles. A slasher waits for you behind the next page. A ghost between words. And there's Sadie Hartmann, too. Here in full. And is there anything better than witnessing a friend pulling it off? Because that's what's happened here. A brilliant woman wrote the exact book she was meant to write at the exact right moment in time.

Welcome.

To modern horror, yes. But to the world, the thoughts, the palate of Sadie Hartmann, too.

–Josh Malerman

Introduction

Forgive me for the title of this book. It used to be *101 Horror Books to Read Before You Die*, but you might live a very long, satisfying life and have plenty of time to read a lot of horror books. Where's the tension in that?

But *101 Horror Books to Read Before You're Murdered*? Now that's horror, baby! And that, my friend, is what we're here for. (Please read the last two sentences as the character George Costanza from *Seinfeld*.)

Now, who is compiling this very important, official-sounding list? Me. Sadie Hartmann, otherwise known as "Mother Horror" on social media. The magical thing that makes me qualified to create a list like this is that I'm a scaredy cat. I know that sounds counterintuitive. A scaredy cat compiling a list of horror fiction books with authority sounds ridiculous, but after I explain some things, it will make all the sense in the world. You will trust my horror book choices implicitly.

I live an extremely timid, unadventurous life. I always have. I'm very sensible and safeguard my well-being at all costs or against any kind of fun. I have an impressive number of fears and phobias, and I very rarely watch scary movies. I do not live deliciously (buuuut I actually did see **that** movie and liked it).

However, there is one profound way I do take risks: I read a metric ton of horror fiction.

I promote it on social media. I buy and sell it through Night Worms, the horror fiction subscription business I co-own. I review it in magazines and on various websites and platforms. I write about it. Photograph it. Curate it. Publish it. Hoard it.

Eat. . .

Drink. . .

Breathe. . .

Well, you get the idea.

I've always been a horror fiction fan. Even before I knew what I was looking for, the grim, macabre, spooky books found me.

My mother is an avid reader with a large library. She gave me unrestrained access to her shelves. Although I wasn't sure if that included her adult "scary books," I still snuck Stephen King books up to my room and read them late into the night like it was a big secret. *Salem's Lot* was my first.

Is this where I get to talk about how Stephen King has changed my life?

* Stares off into space for several minutes . . . *

Stephen King has made a huge impact on my life. Of all the influential celebrities and famous people out there in the world, Stephen King is the one. My hero. Reading his books formed all of my future preferences in literature and influenced all of my biases toward very specific tropes and story-telling styles. He is the reason I gravitate toward horror centered around child protagonists: Danny from *The Shining*, The Loser's Club from *IT*, the brothers in *Eyes of the Dragon*, Jake from The Dark Tower series, Jack from *The Talisman*, and the friend group in *The Body*—which was adapted into my all-time favorite movie, *Stand by Me*.

These characters are immortal in my soul, in my reader's heart. They're always with me. Nothing compares to coming-of-age horror, to growing emotionally attached to a child protagonist on their journey toward adulthood while facing impossible evil.

If you are familiar with the genre of horror, you know Stephen King. Love his books or not, you know them. That's why you won't find any King books on this list. Chances are you've already read my favorites, and if you haven't, you have your reasons. In my opinion, his books are the blueprints for horror. Everything in the genre that has come after builds on the framework he has built. He's the cornerstone of modern horror and my Constant Storyteller.

Horror is so alive at this moment. And five minutes from now, it will be stronger than it is right now. Stand in one place and you can hear it evolving, transforming, shedding its skin over and over and over again. It emerges from its scaled casing a newer creation than it was before with a fire burning in its belly for more growth, more boundaries to cross, more wrongs to right. Horror is relentless in its efforts to reach the hearts of readers and win new souls to the genre.

What an exciting time to be a fan.

There are at least a dozen traditionally published horror books released each month and perhaps double or triple that amount from the small press market. Not to mention whatever the indie authors release themselves. It's impossible to keep up. I caution against even trying. But what a wonderful problem to have. Too many horror books? What a delicious prospect. With so many books to choose from, how can a discerning reader know what to buy? This book is going to cover that. Stay with me. We're going in.

It doesn't matter if you're brand new to the horror genre or if you have been reading it your whole life. This book was written with you in mind. And it probably goes without saying, but I feel like I have to be clear: Nobody is the last word on good horror books. Taste is so supremely subjective. All I can do—all anyone can do—is make honest recommendations on what they feel is quality horror and hope that others will read it and enjoy

it too. So read this book with a grain of salt. Your all-time favorite horror book might not be in here. I either didn't read it or didn't like it or thought something else was better. You're not wrong. I'm not wrong. But I do think narrowing down all of the available titles from the last twenty years or so into a more manageable list of books that should not be missed is essential.

Also, please read horror with a love for yourself and your boundaries. You can research content warnings before you begin a new book to know if any of your specific triggers might arise. And if one escapes your notice and you encounter that trigger, it's OK to stop reading the book. I know some people either feel like they're not allowed to quit on a book or feel guilty about stopping, but this is me telling you that the permission to quit has been granted.

HOW TO READ THIS BOOK

This is a modern horror list. Almost everything included is from 2000–2023. Recency bias? Yes. This is a list of horror **right now**.

There are maybe a bazillion lists on the internet of iconic "must-read" horror. I just Googled "Must-Read Horror Books" and the lists generally include books from all time. I could list off the top of my head at least 50-100 books that will be on those lists. I don't want to make an "All Time" list. It's redundant, and the books that would have to be on that list would squeeze out horror happening right now. More important, you don't have time to go back that far in the annals of history, read all of those books, **and** keep up with what's coming out in today's market before you're murdered.

This book is your jumping-off point into horror **right now**. You can use it to catch up and then stay current from here on out. I want it to be a guidebook on your journey into a genre where the landscape is shifting like sand. Consider me your footpath through horror, leading you to unlocking the best possible experience so you can establish what you love and don't love and make future book purchases with all of this 101 knowledge informing those decisions. (And this is by no means a definitive "Top 100" list of the BEST HORROR OF THE LAST 20 YEARS; otherwise, you know, I would call it that.)

I'll prepare you now: *House of Leaves* by Mark Z. Danielewski isn't on here, and neither is *Let the Right One In* by John Ajvide Lindqvist. I didn't enjoy them, so I don't recommend them. These recommendations are books that I think offer great representations of where horror has been, where it is now, and where it's going. Your "catch up" list before you . . . you know . . . *slicing throat gesture*

I've categorized, sorted, broken down, labeled, and curated this list with you in mind. You can read every word, every recommendation cover-to-cover, or you can look at each book "at a glance." You can skip to the subgenres that interest you the most or find the horror books with a specific tone—there are lots of ways to read this book. These books are organized by theme, but they are not ranked or in any particular order.

Included in this list are ten Author Spotlights. These are authors that I feel represent the genre well and have written so many good books, I couldn't possibly just pick one of their books! I've read and enjoyed several books by each of these authors. Anytime they release a new book, I scramble to get an advance reader's copy, preorder a first edition for my library, and make sure everyone I know that loves horror is informed of the upcoming release. They're pillars in the genre. In these spotlights are books I've read and recommend, as well as other titles by them, with a brief description so you can choose any of their books that sound interesting to you to fill in that spot. (And just to make sure you never run out of recommendations, each author has included three of their very own favorite horror books!)

Additionally, this book would not be a true reflection of me and my taste in horror fiction if it didn't include short story collections. I strongly believe that short fiction is the best format for horror. Authors who are skilled in this discipline manage to maintain heightened suspense, tension, and horror for the duration of the short story. An author's collection is the best way to get to know their storytelling voice so that you can go back and buy novels with similar subgenres or tropes that you enjoyed in their shorter works.

In the back of the book, you'll find even more ways to gather horror for your library.

::Someone raises their hand::

Yes, you in the back row. Do you have a question?

::They stand up::

"So all of the books on this list are scary, right? You picked these books because they're scary?"

No. I'm not sure any of these books will be scary for you or anyone else in this room. What scares us is as unique to ourselves as our fingerprints. We all move through this life with individual experiences that are special to us—nobody lives the same life you do. What you find to be scary is based on the way you engage and interact with this world, and that's different from the way I do it, or anyone else does it.

I would never hold up a horror book and say, "This isn't horror because it's not scary." I don't think a horror book's main objective is to be scary. There are lots of other ways writers can tell stories to unsettle our souls.

I also believe every book probably has an audience that will love it, so I don't want to hinder a book from finding its audience. In the same way, I would never guarantee a book will scare someone. Some people are really hard to scare. However, I do let people know which books have made me leave the lights on. The books on this list are to be considered nightmare fuel with the potential to fan your fears into flame.

AT A GLANCE REFERENCE GUIDE

Every recommendation in this book comes with an At A Glance section designed to help you find your next horror read with as much information as possible in the shortest amount of time. I drew inspiration for these sections from the public library resource NoveList Plus. You can learn more about NoveList Plus on page 161. Below you'll find more details about the Icons, Tones, and Styles I've included in the "At a Glance" sections, but you'll also find Themes, Settings, and Publishers for each book. The Themes often double as trigger warnings, so if you don't like having too many specific details about the book before you read, skip the Themes.

ICONS

BOOK TO MOVIE: the book has been adapted for film or television

CITY LIFE: the characters live in an urban setting

COMING-OF-AGE: one or more of the characters are going through a growing-up phase

COSMIC: the vast universe, human insignificance, Lovecraftian influences or mythos

CRIME NOIR: stylistic crime mysteries in an urban setting; dark and bleak

CULTS!: anything and everything to do with cults and cultish behavior

DARK ACADEMIA: academia and/or takes place primarily at a campus involving students

DARK FANTASY: the opposite of whimsical, lighthearted fantasy

FOUND MEDIA: involves manuscripts, letters, ancient tomes, lost VHS tapes, cassettes, or film

GOTHIC: prevailing atmosphere of mystery and terror

GROSS OUT: graphic/descriptive scenes of bloody carnage, bodily fluids, and/or other nastiness

HAUNTED HOUSE: Home NOT Sweet Home; bad house; scary house; evil house

HISTORICAL FICTION: a real time in history usually depicting an actual event or real people

HUMAN MONSTERS: the villain of the story is us, not anything supernatural or paranormal

INSPIRED BY TRUE EVENTS: involves true crime

LOCKED-ROOM: some kind of trapped situation; isolation

META-FICTION: the author involves himself in the story or breaks the fourth wall

MIND-BENDER: these stories hurt your brain; intricately plotted; twisty-turny

MODERN WESTERN: not your grandpa's Western books

MYSTERY: a primary aspect to the horror is a mystery of some kind, usually murder

PSYCHOLOGICAL: the characters go through psychological trauma

READS LIKE A THRILLER: thriller/horror mash-ups

RELIGIOUS STUFF: introduces religious themes, bible verses, organized religion, people of faith

SMALL TOWN HORROR: set in a small town

SOUTHERN GOTHIC: a specifically Southern form of Gothic horror

GRL
PWR **STRONG WOMEN:** the female protagonists are strong and kick ass

SURVIVAL: people alone or in groups surviving tough situations

HORROR TONES

ATMOSPHERIC: a distinctive mood felt throughout the experience

BLEAK: hopelessness

BLOOD-SOAKED: descriptive or detailed violence; carnage

BRUTAL: savage violence

DARK: heavy subject matter

DISORIENTING: intentionally confuses the reader

DISTURBING: causes anxiety, fear, revulsion

EERIE: strange and frightening

GRUESOME: repulsive or unpleasant scenes

HUMOROUS: funny, witty, clever

INTENSIFYING DREAD: a slow building sense of bad things coming

MELANCHOLY: a constant feeling of sadness and turmoil

MENACING: a threatening presence of danger

SHOCKING: unexpected events

SUSPENSEFUL: uncertainty about what may happen

VIOLENT: physical harm and death

STYLES

ABSTRACT: boundless and limitless; not beholden to concrete laws of nature

BRISK PACING: events lead to action scenes; story moves quickly; cliffhangers

CHARACTER-DRIVEN: emphasis on character experience over plot-driven storytelling

CINEMATIC: very descriptive/detailed; cinematic in nature; vivid storytelling

CLIVE BARKER(ISH): when something feels heavily influenced by Barker's style

CRITICALLY ACCLAIMED: received generally good reviews from a number of critics; thought-provoking

DUAL TIMELINE: The story is told from two or more periods of time.

FIRST-PERSON POV (POINT OF VIEW): "I" storytelling from one character

INTRICATELY PLOTTED: complex twists and turns; complicated characters; a lot of moving parts

LEISURELY PACED: "slow burn"; no sense of urgency

LYRICAL: poetic prose

MULTIPLE POV (POINTS OF VIEW): narrative from multiple character points of view

STEPHEN KING(ISH): when something feels heavily influenced by King's style

VIGNETTES: short, sharp, interconnected scenes fused together to form one story (also called mosaic)

PARANORMAL

AS A CHILD, I HATED IT when adults would say, "Goodnight, sleep tight, don't let the bed bugs bite." What a horrible thought to put in a child's head before turning out the lights and leaving them all alone!

Of course, as I got older and started reading adult horror books before bed, I was willingly putting much more terrifying images in my head before drifting off to sleep. But I'll never forget that feeling of wondering if the boogeyman was hiding in my closet or lying in wait under my bed so it could bite me.

I'm going to provide a more textbook explanation of paranormal, but the following traditional Scottish prayer captures my definition of what classifies as paranormal horror pretty well: *"From Ghoulies and Ghoosties, long-leggety Beasties, and Things that go Bump in the Night, Good Lord, deliver us!"*

According to science, everything in the natural world around us can be observed and ultimately explained scientifically after some investigation. Except for that which is *beyond normal*. Abnormal. Paranormal.

In other words, freaky shit that defies explanation. A pretty broad topic.

Some paranormal phenomena include ghosts and poltergeists, haunted houses, psychic abilities, UFOs and aliens, and cryptids (Bigfoot, the Loch Ness Monster, Chupacabra, etc.). All of these strange accounts have the potential to be real, however unlikely, and no matter which way you lean, you're bound to find evidence to support your beliefs.

This is why we all love the *X-Files*, right? The two main paranormal investigators, agents Fox Mulder and Dana Scully, represent the two ways people commonly deal with paranormal phenomena.

Mulder would say the truth is out there and he wants to believe.

And Scully is your classic skeptic: I'll believe it when I see it and I have no other choice.

The words *paranormal* and *supernatural* are sometimes used interchangeably when classifying the specific horror in books, and we'll get into those nuances more in the chapter on supernatural book recommendations. But a great way to keep them straight is to think about Paranormal Romance books—have you seen that section in a bookstore? It's a subset of literature where there is a romance between a human and something paranormal: a vampire, werewolf, ghost, or even—hold on to your butts—a doctor falling in love with the actual Coronavirus and having a sexual relationship with it.

With the virus.

I know. Seems strange, but it has almost nine hundred reviews with a four-star rating so . . . *shrugs*

Haunted Houses

Within, walls continued upright, bricks met neatly, floors were firm, and doors were sensibly shut; silence lay steadily against the wood and stone of Hill House, and whatever walked there, walked alone.

—Shirley Jackson, *The Haunting of Hill House*

So many of us grew up in neighborhoods with that one house. You know the one. Picture it. The dilapidated relic on your street with ratty curtains always drawn, paint peeling, and gutters sagging. A neglected front yard overrun with weeds and thistles. No one goes in. No one goes out. Empty driveway. The lights are never on. There are no signs of life, and yet . . . the house looks abandoned but feels occupied. Haunted. A ghostly presence. But it's just a house, right?

Depends on the house.

Hauntings are a universally held paranormal phenomenon. It's the belief that ghosts or spirits manifest themselves regularly, and in one location. In horror, there are two common types of houses: a "Manderley" house and a "Hill House."

MANDERLEY

Picture the beautiful, large, sprawling estate in Southern England from Daphne du Maurier's book *Rebecca*. The new Mrs. de Winter realizes too late that the ghost of her husband's first wife, Rebecca, is still very much the lady of Manderley. Manderley is the blueprint for stories that ask

the reader, "Is it the house or the people?" Is the Manderley estate haunted by the spirit of a woman refusing to let her husband move on, or are the people of Manderley possessed by the past, unwilling to let Rebecca go? This trope is a well-worn favorite enjoyed time and time again from *Rebecca* to 2022's release, *The Hacienda* by Isabel Cañas (page 26). Is the haunting paranormal or psychological?

HILL HOUSE

This is the quintessential Gothic haunted house, complete with a horrible past filled with violence and death. In Shirley Jackson's book *The Haunting of Hill House*, she lays the groundwork for all other haunted house books to follow. Hill House is dangerous. The house is a supernatural entity that can, if it chooses to do so, take the life of anyone that enters it. In fact, I would assume that it desires to do so. It can be said that those who sleep in its beds or wander its halls do not leave in the same condition as when they arrived.

Iconic, fictional haunted houses have already set the precedents, and these recommendations live up to that standard in their own unique way.

THE GRIP OF IT

BY JAC JEMC (2017)

What role were we playing?
The ghosts or the haunted?

Oh goodness. Some tropes never get old. I love it when a young married couple decides to move into a new house to fix all their problems. A change of pace. A new start.

Seasoned couples already know: Buying and moving into a new home are stressors that add to existing problems, not fix them! But it sure is entertaining to watch fictional couples figure it out for themselves.

Julie and James leave their urban landscape and head for a more rural address, moving into a new house at the edge of a dense forest. They bring with them big expectations for a change of scenery to inspire a fresh start for their struggling relationship. Almost immediately, strange things begin to happen. Jemc uses a back-and-forth, his-and-hers narrative to keep readers guessing about what's going on as both Julie and James seem to have different experiences. The chapters are succinct, often leaving readers on a cliffhanger. The pages fly by like a little movie in the reader's mind. I love the way the author leaves room for the audience to develop theories.

Perhaps the most rewarding part of this book is that no two readers will have the same experience. There will be paranormal skeptics who run with clues suggesting one thing, while other readers will lean into the unexplained phenomena to propose a different reality. Either way, my recommendation would be to buddy-read this with a friend and compare notes and theories along the way.

Those who are not fans of ambiguity might feel the need for concrete answers, but it's the psychological disturbance of the unknown that makes this book one of my favorites in the subgenre.

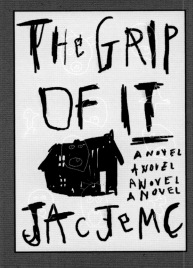

AT A GLANCE

A "Manderley" House

THEMES: Moving into a new house, marriage and marital secrets, creepy woods, unreliable narrators, gambling, trust issues, possession, suspicion, isolation

TONE: Atmospheric, Eerie, Dark, Disorienting, Intensifying Dread, Menacing, Suspenseful

STYLE: Character-Driven, First-Person POV, Intricately Plotted, Leisurely Paced, Multiple POV

SETTING: Upstate New York

PUBLISHER: Traditional/FSG

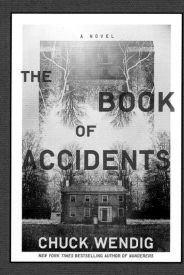

AT A GLANCE

A "Hill House"

THEMES: Family, love, art, empaths, child abuse, bullies, good vs. evil, hometown, demonic powers, dark magic, paranormal phenomena

TONE: Intensifying Dread, Menacing, Suspenseful

STYLE: Character-Driven, Stephen King(ish)

SETTING: Pennsylvania

PUBLISHER: Traditional/ Del Rey Books

THE BOOK OF ACCIDENTS

BY CHUCK WENDIG (2021)

In horror's wake, hope was a bountiful garden.

I enjoy that horror fiction has the potential to be emotionally devastating. In the hands of the right author, a story will pull the reader into the lives of fictional characters wholly and completely, creating a very real, heartfelt connection. When horror or trauma is introduced, threatening those fictional lives, it's almost unbearable for the reader.

<Chuck Wendig enters the chat>

I went into *The Book of Accidents* with full knowledge of Wendig's penchant for emotional wreckage (I'm a huge fan of his *Miriam Black* series), and that's really what I show up for. He did not disappoint.

A family of three—Nate, Maddie, and their son Oliver—move back to Nate's childhood home where he experienced trauma at the hands of his father. Maddie experienced childhood trauma in this same town as well, so both parents are feeling cautious and protective regarding their son Oliver, who has been struggling socially at school as an emotionally fragile empath.

I fell in love with this family. My heart was especially drawn to Oliver because he reminded me of my teenage son. So, as soon as Oliver makes a mysterious new friend who gives off a lot of red flags, my mom instincts went into full panic mode—a true sign of great horror. All those feelings!

Chuck Wendig's storytelling style is uniquely accessible and compelling, like a best friend telling you a great story. His wheelhouse is reaching past the page to grab his audience's emotions. This book will run you through a full gamut of feelings, but the primary emphasis is on the power of love as our best resource against impossible evil and darkness. And this does get dark, but it never loses sight of hope.

JUST LIKE HOME

BY SARAH GAILEY (2022)

Is one possible without the other? I think you have to know someone in order to truly love them, and you have to love someone in order to really hate them.

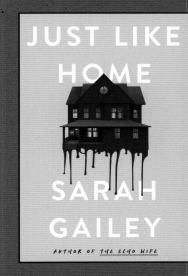

This book instantly rocketed to my all-time favorite list of horror books because it ticks every single box. The writing is impeccable, engaging, and provocative. You must go into this book with little knowledge of the plot. I beg you.

After being summoned by her estranged mother who is dying, Vera returns home and encounters flashbacks of her thirteen-year-old self in the same house struggling through a difficult childhood.

That's it. I'd like to preserve your reading discoveries at all costs because that's exactly how I was able to engage with this book, and it served me well. Reviews are going to give too much away. The less you know, the better. Having said that, I will drop some subtle clues in the "At a Glance" section that do double duty as themes and trigger warnings.

Just Like Home is the future of horror. The direction we're heading toward. It's whipcrack smart, intricately plotted, and fluctuates perfectly between a past and present narrative. The characters are complex—each serving a purpose to further the horror embedded in this tale. Nobody is an afterthought or an add-on. Every line of dialogue develops layers upon layers of nuance. Gailey's insidious brand of supernatural terror effortlessly works together with psychological elements to create a hybrid thriller–horror rollercoaster that I could have ridden on into oblivion. What a dark, delicious, seductive book. I'll never get over it, and it's forever on my book recommendation list.

AT A GLANCE
A "Manderley" House

THEMES: Mothers and daughters, daughters and fathers, jealousy, dysfunctional families, serial killers, scandal, generational sin, neglected children, basements, trauma, wickedness, a parent dying, homecoming

TONE: Disturbing, Gruesome, Intensifying Dread

STYLE: Dual Timeline, Intricately Plotted

SETTING: Upstate New York

PUBLISHER: Traditional/ Tor Books

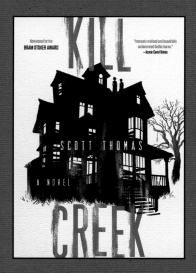

KILL CREEK

BY SCOTT THOMAS (2017)

There it was, the house on Kill Creek, the Finch House, the old, grizzled monster that stalked the dreams of children, that danced on the tongues of morbid storytellers.

Kill Creek reads like a love letter to horror fiction fans. It's like Scott Thomas made a list of everything horror fans show up for and set out to deliver it all in one haunted house book.

Four authors, all famous in their own right, are invited to spend Halloween night together at the notorious Finch House for a publicity stunt. A quirky internet mogul is their host for the evening's festivities. It has a very similar setup to some of horror's most timeless tales: Shirley Jackson's *The Haunting of Hill House*, Agatha Christie's *And Then There Were None*, and Richard Matheson's *Hell House*.

The author gives plenty of backstory about each character before turning them loose on each other for the duration of their experience at Finch House. But there's another entity invited to this sleepover that wasn't mentioned: Finch House. And the house is not amused.

Plenty of spectral encounters and ghastly mayhem ensues, ramping up until its final, bloody, high-energy conclusion. Some books are just fun. Like buying tickets to an action movie that you know is not trying too hard to win all the Oscars but is just honestly hell-bent on delivering exactly what the audience craves. That's *Kill Creek*. All the stereotypes, all the tropes, and all the iconic vibes are smooshed into one story. Part modern psychological thriller, part old-school horror, this book is a good time from beginning to end.

AT A GLANCE

A "Hill House"

THEMES: Halloween night, horror authors, internet stunts, folklore and legend, abandoned houses

TONE: Atmospheric, Gruesome, Suspenseful

STYLE: Brisk Pacing, Character-Driven

SETTING: Kansas

PUBLISHER: Indie/Inkshares

THE ANCESTOR

BY DANIELLE TRUSSONI (2020)

The mind is like warm wax, the world like a brass seal pressed into it. Such imprints are forever stamped into us. I am eternally marred.

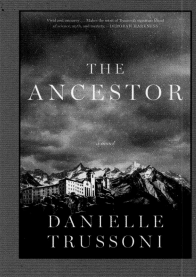

I have never wanted to live in the pages of a horror novel as much as I did while reading *The Ancestor*.

Alberta Montebianco lives a stressful, emotionally complicated lifestyle in New York. With almost magical timing, a letter shows up addressed to her, but with a new title in front of her name: "Countess." As it turns out, Alberta discovers that she is possibly the sole living heir to a noble title and a castle in Turin, Italy.

The perfect setup for a compelling story. I felt like I was reading the source material for an old black-and-white movie starring a classic Hollywood silver-screen beauty. All of the chapters with Trussoni's bewildered protagonist exploring her new digs in Italy are life-giving, fairytale-esque magic. I loved all the detailed, descriptive language of the castle and decor.

But is it horror? Sounds a bit dreamy.

Just know this: It would be almost impossible to imagine at the start of this book where it ultimately ends up. Horror fans, if you enjoy a well-crafted Gothic tale, this book is a must!

AT A GLANCE

A "Manderley" House

GRL PWR

THEMES: Inheritance, wealthy families, royalty, family secrets and history, death

TONE: Atmospheric, Eerie, Intensifying Dread, Suspenseful

STYLE: Character-Driven, Cinematic, Critically Acclaimed, Leisurely Paced

SETTING: Italy

PUBLISHER: Traditional/ William Morrow

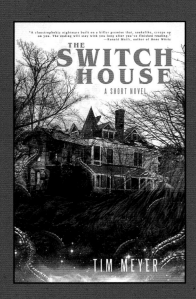

THE SWITCH HOUSE
BY TIM MEYER (2018)

She realizes she's looking the elements of space and time in the face and her mind feels like a cheap piece of glass ready to break, ready to crumble, ready to cut and draw blood.

The Switch House is the book that opened my eyes to the talent pool within the self-published market. About halfway through my reading experience, I realized I had unlocked a new level in my quest to read everything the genre had to offer.

This is a slick, lean, and mean novella, with virtually no wasted space here as Meyer intentionally streamlined this story to pack a violent punch.

My recommendation is to make sure you have the time to read this in one sitting because you're not going to want to put this down. Meyer expertly develops a small cast of characters in a matter of a few pages and then throws down the gauntlet. The horrors stack up at an unrelenting pace, each fresh scare building the tension to the perfect climax. I was legitimately frightened 30 percent into the book, and I knew it had the potential to make me not want to turn the lights off or forget to close my closet door. This story is original with powerful twists and turns. I immediately wanted to read it again as soon as I finished to see if I missed any signposts.

The Switch House is fast and fierce. Probably the best example of how shorter works of fiction are so effective at maintaining horror tension all the way through.

AT A GLANCE

A "Hill House"

GRL PWR

THEMES: Reality TV and TV stars, home, nightmares, delusions, reality, therapy, perceived reality, marriage, hallucinations, murder, pregnancy, miscarriage, love

TONE: Blood-Soaked, Brutal, Disorienting, Melancholy, Menacing

STYLE: Brisk Pacing, Character-Driven, Cinematic, Clive Barker(ish), Intricately Plotted

SETTING: New Jersey

PUBLISHER: Indie/Evil Epoch Press

Match these Fictional Writers to Their Stephen King Story

MIKE NOONAN	*LISEY'S STORY*
PAUL SHELDON	*"SECRET WINDOW, SECRET GARDEN"*
SCOTT LANDON	*"1408"*
JACK TORRANCE	*BAG OF BONES*
MORT RAINEY	*THE DARK HALF*
GORDIE LACHANCE	*THE SHINING*
BEN MEARS	*MISERY*
GEORGE STARK	*SALEM'S LOT*
MIKE ENSLIN	*THE BODY*

Match Each Haunted House to its Author

29 NEIBOLT ST	MARK DANIELEWSKI
HILL HOUSE	JONATHAN JANZ
BLY MANOR	DAPHNE DU MAURIER
MANDERLEY	KEALAN PATRICK BURKE
THE HOUSE ON ASH TREE LANE	SHIRLEY JACKSON
ALEXANDER HOUSE	HENRY JAMES
56 ABIGAIL LANE	STEPHEN KING

Christopher Buehlman

Let's make this a little interactive. Go to my Goodreads review of the book *Between Two Fires* by Christopher Buehlman and look at the twenty updates I did while I was reading it. In a nutshell, it's just me fangirling into oblivion in real time.

That book is a game-changer. An honest-to-god life-altering book; the kind that becomes a new gold standard by which everything else is measured and comes up quite short. I was pissed that I had never heard of it before. What the fuck is everyone out there doing with their lives that they haven't read the greatest medieval, dark fantasy, character-driven horror novel of all time? When this book ended, I sat alone in my living room and fell apart. Maybe the most emotional I have been since the last book in The Dark Tower series by Stephen King.

After *Between Two Fires*, I bought more of Buehlman's books and immediately read *The Lesser Dead*, which is a vampire novel, and *Those Across the River*, a werewolf novel. It's mind-blowing how all three books are so completely different from one another. The storytelling voice in *Between Two Fires* resonates with the era in which it takes place. You want to wrap yourself in a big, thick blanket on a stone hearth in front of a roaring fire while someone reads to you from this book before bedtime. There's a storm outside, no electricity, and the room is dark.

In stark contrast to that atmosphere is *The Lesser Dead* and its narrator's voice, Joey Peacock. He speaks right to you. He sees you. He desires to tell about his life as a vampire and specifically about this particular event that changes everything for him and his "family" of vampires who live in a community underground in New York City during the late 1970s. Peacock's voice is intoxicating—with so much personality and swagger—I was immediately captivated by him.

Those Across the River takes place in Georgia during the Great Depression. The pace is steamy, leisurely. A broad-shouldered, handsome professor takes up with a colleague's hot wife and the two of them skip off to a small town. They settle into their new house by enjoying afternoon delights and going out after the heat of the day to get acquainted with the townsfolk, who often warn them not to go off into the woods alone. I'm for sure not going to tell you anything else—just read it. Since nobody told me about Christopher Buehlman, I'm being a good friend and making sure you stock your shelves with his books and actually read them. You're welcome.

RECOMMENDED TITLES

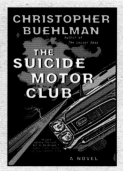

BETWEEN TWO FIRES (2012)
medieval; dark fantasy; paranormal

THE LESSER DEAD (2014)
paranormal; vampire

THOSE ACROSS THE RIVER (2011)
paranormal; werewolves; Southern Gothic

THE SUICIDE MOTOR CLUB (2016)
paranormal; vampires; hunter–hunted

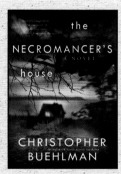

THE NECROMANCER'S HOUSE (2013)
paranormal; witches; warlocks; dark fantasy

THE BLACKTONGUE THIEF (2021)
high, dark fantasy

Christopher Buehlman Recommends: "I'll start with Shirley Jackson's masterpiece, *The Haunting of Hill House*. If you haven't got bags under your eyes after that protagonist gets psychologically bullied by the malicious dead, I'll send you off with Adam Nevill's insomniac chiller *Last Days* to see how you fare with the "Old Friends." If you return from those strange shores intact, I'll turn you over to *The Exorcist*. But you won't be reading it — author William Peter Blatty narrates the audiobook, and you'll be listening to that, alone, in a dark house where maybe, if you're very lucky, rats have moved into the attic."

Ghosts

If there are ghosts, what do they want? Are they benign? Are they evil? Are they here to exact revenge (justified or not), to take care of unfinished business that was interrupted by a violent death, or because they're prevented from resting by the living? And are there places haunted by the echoes of those who lived and died in them?

—Ellen Datlow, introduction to *Echoes*

Remember the sleepover party game, Truth or Dare? One time, at my friend Mara's overnight birthday party, we played it after her parents said it was time for lights out. The truth-telling was silly and the dares were harmless, until one girl dared us all to play Bloody Mary in the bathroom.

Shit got serious real quick.

Did I mention Mara lived in a haunted house? Her family chose—willingly—to live in our small town's historically preserved hospital. There was no chance in hell I was going to participate in conjuring up a legendary evil spirit in a haunted house that was already known for its ghost stories.

It's important for me to make some distinctions about different kinds of ghosts. At my friend's house, people talked about hearing a baby crying in the room that used to be the maternity ward or seeing an apparition on the staircase. Those are your garden variety ghosts that are relatively harmless. But there are poltergeists too. These restless entities can make physical contact with objects or people. They can open doors, move furniture, break glass, and maybe even injure people. Dangerous. Menacing. For me, it's all terrifying. I don't want to wake up and see a ghost in my bedroom and wonder if it's just an apparition or if it has the ability to harm me, so all ghosts are scary and should be considered threatening. I don't want to encounter them in real life, but I do want to read about them.

It's enjoyable to watch from a safe distance what could happen to fictional people when they encounter a vengeful poltergeist hell-bent on destroying the lives of the living. Afterward, the book gets shelved, and you get to go about your ghost-free existence. Unless, of course, the nightmare fuel lingers and you wind up sleeping with one eye open and the light on. You'll have to read these recommendations to find out.

HEART-SHAPED BOX

BY JOE HILL (2007)

He understood that the ghost existed first and foremost within his own head. That maybe ghosts always haunted minds, not places.

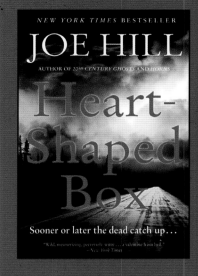

I recommend this book to readers who ask, "What's the scariest book you've ever read?" This is one of them.

Jude Coyne is a semi-retired rock star living his best life with his girlfriend and a couple of dogs. One of his favorite hobbies is collecting cursed objects and oddities, which leads him to purchase a haunted suit off the internet. How bad of an idea is this? I love how right away, readers are like, "This is not going to end well for Jude."

The suit arrives in a heart-shaped box. Opening it releases a malignant spirit that can influence the living to commit heinous acts. After the suit's arrival, curious things begin happening, which begs the question: Did Jude just happen upon finding this suit through the internet, or was the suit *pursuing* Jude? Discovering the answer to this question is a terrifying experience.

The descriptions of the ghost leap off the page. While I was reading, I would look around the room to make sure I was alone. Do not read this book if you're home alone at night, or if you want a good night's sleep.

Jude Coyne's character arc is especially noteworthy. The trauma he endures during the book is a catalyst for personal growth in his relationships and an opportunity to see life differently. *Heart-Shaped Box* is the perfect modern-day ghost story.

AT A GLANCE

THEMES: Cursed objects, rock stars/celebrities, oddities, the internet, seances, vengeance, pure evil

TONE: Blood-Soaked, Disturbing, Gruesome, Intensifying Dread

STYLE: Brisk Pacing, Character-Driven, Cinematic, Intricately Plotted, Stephen King(ish)

SETTING: Upstate New York

PUBLISHER: Traditional/ William Morrow

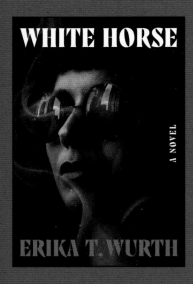

WHITE HORSE

BY ERIKA T. WURTH (2022)

A sound like bones cracking came from her limbs, and abruptly, she moved jerkily a few inches in my direction, her head still down — she raised her head up sharply, her eyes white, her mouth pouring blood, and screamed.

Horror meets crime thriller is the perfect combination. It's got all the page-turning excitement of unlocking secrets to solve the case, but with the atmosphere of bone-chilling horror.

This is a modern ghost story centered on the female experience; more specifically, a twenty-first-century Indigenous female experience. Kari wants to someday own her favorite dive bar, White Horse. She's single, carefree, rocks out to metal music, and reads Stephen King. Her best friend and cousin, Debby, surprises her one night with an old bracelet she found belonging to Kari's deceased mother. When Kari touches it, the visions start.

Haunted by the past, Kari goes on a quest to learn more about her mother's strange disappearance and possible murder. This journey draws her back to her Native American heritage and estranged family members. Peppered throughout this supernatural murder mystery are some exceptionally well-written scenes focusing on identity. The two women, Kari and Debby, independently struggle to establish agency.

Debby is clearly on a path of erasure. Her sense of self is tied to her controlling husband who insists on making important life-altering decisions for her. Kari is in a constant state of moving forward to accomplish goals, then taking two steps back with self-sabotaging behavior. She wrestles with her traditional Native upbringing and the Urban Native she has become.

The Native American lore chasing Kari in the form of the Lofa, a monstrous ogre that preys on women, works in tandem with the distressed ghost of her mother to create an element of urgency and tension that carries throughout the entire reading experience. A thrilling horror debut from Erika T. Wurth.

AT A GLANCE

THEMES: Best friends, death of a parent, estranged family, murder mystery, haunted, folklore, Native American culture

TONE: Brutal, Intensifying Dread, Melancholy, Menacing

STYLE: Brisk Pacing, Character-Driven, Cinematic, Critically Acclaimed, Intricately Plotted

SETTING: Denver, CO

PUBLISHER: Traditional/ Flatiron Books

WHEN THE RECKONING COMES

BY LATANYA MCQUEEN (2021)

Hush though, and listen. If you're quiet, you can hear their whispers in the water calling to those left behind. Hush and you can hear them lurking, waiting for the day they can make their return.

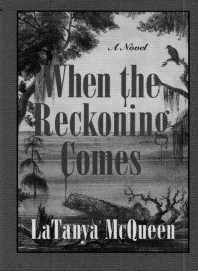

LaTanya McQueen follows in the footsteps of Toni Morrison's *Beloved*, infusing social commentary about the horrors of slavery with a haunting, fictional ghost story.

A young woman named Mira returns to the town she grew up in to attend the wedding of a childhood friend. The venue is a tobacco plantation, The Woodsman House, which is tied up with Mira's personal history. She is shocked to learn that the plantation has been renovated into a tourist attraction, complete with African Americans in roles of servitude. It's uncomfortable to visualize the era of enslavement romanticized in a modern, public venue. As the wedding ceremony draws near, Mira is increasingly haunted by horrible, graphic visions of the Woodsman plantation's violent history and visited by restless, vengeful spirits. Mira's transformation from just a casual observer to becoming a supernatural conduit is concerning. It never really leaves your mind.

While the subject matter here is extremely disturbing and detailed, LaTanya McQueen balances it out with lighthearted banter between friends. I love when characters return to their hometowns after several years and seek out old flames. It's so entertaining to be a fly on the wall as emotional history is rekindled.

I enjoyed how the book sustained a level of tension throughout by prompting the reader to consider which is worse: the evil that mankind inflicts on one another or the "reckoning coming," as suggested by the title. It's the perfect blend of haunted house horror tropes with the pacing of a thriller.

AT A GLANCE

THEMES: Slavery, vivid dreams, visions of the past, returning home, plantations, antebellum era, racism, revenge, friendship, running from the past, destination weddings

TONE: Blood-Soaked, Brutal, Eerie, Gruesome, Menacing, Shocking, Violent

STYLE: Brisk Pacing, Character-Driven, Cinematic, Intricately Plotted, Multiple POV

SETTING: N/A

PUBLISHER: Traditional/ Harper Perennial

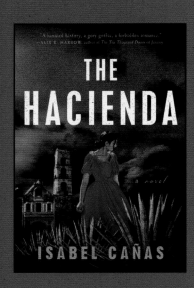

THE HACIENDA

BY ISABEL CAÑAS (2022)

Tending to lost souls is my vocation, Dona Beatriz.

There should be more romance in horror. There, I said it. We make music about love, and we sing about love. Love is everywhere and an integral part of who we are as human beings, so love should be in our horror too.

The Hacienda is a historical, Gothic, horror romance. It takes place in the aftermath of the Mexican War of Independence. A woman named Beatriz and her widowed mother are forced to live with family after the war claimed Beatriz's father's life. Unsatisfied with her station in life, Beatriz sets her sights on a handsome man, Don Rodolfo, with a large estate. Smitten with Beatriz at a party, he proposes and whisks her off to make his house her home. She soon realizes that the rumors surrounding his wife's untimely death and the way the estate makes her feel might be connected.

The estate is haunted by her husband's first wife. A woman wronged.

Beatriz is alone with this vengeful spirit while her husband is off doing whatever it is that he does, and she finally seeks help from a (handsome) young priest. There's much more to Padre Andrés than meets the eye. Together, Beatriz and Andrés investigate the history of Hacienda San Isidro, the secrets of Don Rodolfo Solózano's first marriage, and their deepening relationship. This book fires on all cylinders, satisfying multiple horror cravings. This story is everything I want out of horror. Whenever I pick this book up, I am immersed in its atmosphere. I am there.

AT A GLANCE

THEMES: Love, marriage, religious influences, socioeconomic dynamic, witchcraft, cultural superstitions, classism, sibling rivalry, murder mystery

TONE: Atmospheric, Intensifying Dread, Suspenseful

STYLE: Character-Driven, Cinematic, Intricately Plotted, Leisurely Paced, Multiple POV

SETTING: 1820s Mexico

PUBLISHER: Traditional/ Berkley

Get in the Holiday "Spirit"!

Telling ghost stories has to be one of the oldest oral traditions we have. In the Victorian era, after Christmas dinner, families would gather in the parlor by the fire and tell ghost stories. The most infamous one is *A Christmas Carol*, but if you're interested in carrying on that tradition, I recommend the annual *Valancourt Book of Victorian Christmas Ghost Stories*. They have five volumes now. Let's rekindle this tradition and enjoy ghost stories as a way to get in the holiday spirit!
Here are a few recommendations:

VALANCOURT VICTORIAN GHOST STORIES VOLUMES 1–5

THE SHRIEKING SKULL & OTHER VICTORIAN GHOST STORIES
BY JAMES SKIPP BORLASE

HARK! THE HERALD ANGELS SCREAM ANTHOLOGY
EDITED BY CHRISTOPHER GOLDEN

SEASONS CREEPINGS BY RONALD KELLY

NOS4A2 BY JOE HILL

WRAITH BY JOE HILL

KRAMPUS: THE YULE LORD BY GERALD BROM

SECRET SANTA BY ANDREW SHAFFER

THE VISITOR BY SERGIO GOMEZ

DEAD OF WINTER BY KEALAN PATRICK BURKE

HALLDARK HOLIDAYS EDITED BY GABINO IGLESIAS

WHERE THE DEAD GO TO DIE BY
MARK ALLAN GUNNELLS AND AARON DRIES

Tananarive Due

Due's wheelhouse is developing flesh and blood characters through authentic dialogue. I love how she takes the time to place characters in the day-to-day, mundane settings, like the family dinner table, a husband and wife getting ready for bed, and people driving or doing laundry—all while seamlessly blending in elements of the supernatural, the African diaspora, and human evil.

I recommend starting with Due's short story collection, *Ghost Summer*. Each story is a showcase of Due's ability to draw readers into a provocative narrative across a variety of subgenres. A remarkable aspect of this collection is Due's obvious love of history. It doesn't matter if she is writing a dystopian, science fiction, or apocalyptic tale—historical elements are present. Equally important in *Ghost Summer* are the themes of race, the historical and present oppression of African Americans. These are horror stories as told by a Black horror writer in her own voice.

Due also wrestles with themes of death and dying. Through her writing, we struggle with the impossible, overwhelming pain and suffering of loved ones leaving too soon and struggling with the weight of the space where they used to be.

If you're not a fan of short stories, Due's debut novel, *The Between*, is the perfect place to start. It captures everything I love about her writing. There's a bit of the paranormal as the main character's brush with death causes him to have vivid dreams in his adult life that are nightmarish and some of the best, scariest sequences of the book. Another option, *The Good House*, is a haunted house horror story cleverly infused with voodoo magic, demonic possession, and generational family drama.

As an emotional reader that gets overly invested in the lives of fictional characters, I recklessly indulge in Tananarive Due's works even knowing that the subject matter of her stories could destroy me. However, some stories still fill me with hope and optimism.

Photo by Melissa Hibbert

RECOMMENDED TITLES

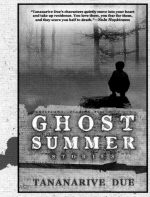

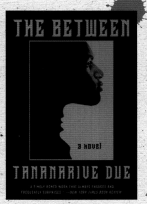

GHOST SUMMER (2015)
short story collection; paranormal; supernatural; sci-fi

THE GOOD HOUSE (2016)
haunted house; supernatural; generational curse

THE BETWEEN (2005)
lucid dreaming; visions; supernatural; stalker

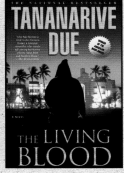

THE AFRICAN IMMORTALS SERIES
follows the lives of mortals and immortals who have contact with Living Blood that can heal any ailment almost instantly. Themes: life, loss, and mortality.

Tananarive Due Recommends: "My three horror books I would include (although somewhat untraditional) are *Beloved* by Toni Morrison, *Kindred* by Octavia E. Butler and *The Only Good Indians* by Stephen Graham Jones."

Creatures & Cryptids

Writing this book with you in mind, Horror Reader, I never want to assume you already know everything there is to know about the genre. That's what leads to gatekeeping. You've seen or maybe even experienced those comments on social media.

Gatekeeper: "I love books about cryptids!"

You: "What's a cryptid?"

Gatekeeper: "If you don't know what a cryptid is, you're not a REAL horror fan."

So, anytime you see a comment like that, your new response is: "*Real horror fans get excited about welcoming new people to the genre.*"

And then just move on because dogs like that never learn new tricks.

A cryptid is a creature or beast that is believed to exist, but has never been scientifically proven to be real. Wikipedia has a great list of cryptids. Living in the Pacific Northwest, I'm partial to stories about our regional monster, Bigfoot a.k.a. Sasquatch, but there are hundreds of cryptids, like the Loch Ness Monster, Mothman, Thunderbird, and The Jersey Devil, just to name a few popular ones.

Creatures of horror are especially celebrated at Halloween, including legendary monsters like vampires and werewolves, as well as mythological creatures like mermaids.

I would also categorize beasts and monsters in this subgenre, with animals gone wild such as *Pearl* by Josh Malerman (page 76), *Cujo* by Stephen King, *Jaws* by Peter Benchly, and *The Rats* by James Herbert.

Quintessential reading in this subgenre includes *Mongrels* by Stephen Graham Jones (page 114), as well as classic horror stories like *Dracula* by Bram Stoker and *Frankenstein* by Mary Shelley. The classics seriously hold up. If you have put off reading them due to their age, let me assure you that they are just as relevant today as they were when they were first released. But if you're feeling that sense of, "Too many books, so little time before I'm murdered," then my selections are all you need to scratch that cryptid itch.

GHOUL

BY BRIAN KEENE (2007)

"Boys have scars," he thought. "Some of them fade and others don't. Some scars stay with us for life."

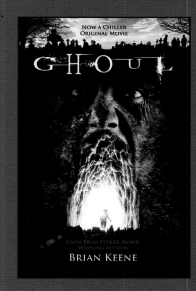

If I've learned anything really important from coming-of-age horror, it's that children are always to be believed—even if they tell you that there is a glowing, naked ghoul hell-bent on impregnating women in its subterranean lair under the town cemetery.

This is the premise for Brian Keene's *Ghoul*.

It's 1984, and three twelve-year-old boys are looking forward to spending the summer in their hidden fort, eating junk food, reading comics, and talking about girls. Things are going according to plan until the boys are faced with having to battle an ancient terror that has taken up residence in their town's cemetery. But even worse than this horny, corpse-eating ghoul are the real-life monsters in their own homes. The up-front emotional investment in the lives of these young boys teetering on adolescence is what turns the horror dial up to full blast. My reader's heart did not want anything bad to happen to them, so when Keene leans into some gut-wrenching terror . . . I could feel my blood pressure rise.

You'll go into this book expecting a creature feature offering only blood and carnage, but you'll close the book with tears in your eyes, your heart torn in two, and a hollow feeling in your guts. That is to say, you'll experience some real feelings, which is the best part of being a horror fan.

Animals Gone Wild!

JURASSIC PARK BY MICHAEL CRICHTON

THE BIRDS BY DAPHNE DU MAURIER

THE CORMORANT BY STEPHEN GREGORY

PET SEMATARY BY STEPHEN KING

HELL HOUND BY KEN GREENHALL

THE UNITED STATES OF CRYPTIDS BY J. W. OCKER

AT A GLANCE

THEMES: Ghouls, teenage boys, summer vacation, friendship, child abuse, family dynamics, small town, graveyards, childhood trauma, sexuality, rape

TONE: Disturbing, Gruesome, Intensifying Dread, Violent

STYLE: Brisk Pacing, Character-Driven, Cinematic, Stephen King(ish)

SETTING: Pennsylvania

PUBLISHER: Traditional/ Leisure Books; Deadite Press (2012)

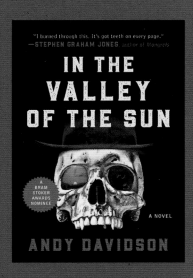

> "I burned through this. It's got teeth on every page."
> —STEPHEN GRAHAM JONES, author of *Mongrels*

IN THE VALLEY OF THE SUN

A NOVEL

ANDY DAVIDSON

A BRAM STOKER AWARDS NOMINEE

AT A GLANCE

GRL PWR

THEMES: Murder, serial killers, vampires, Texas Rangers, running from the law, rural living, single mothers, child abuse, domestic abuse

TONE: Dark, Intensifying Dread, Melancholy

STYLE: Character-Driven, Cinematic, Critically Acclaimed, Leisurely Paced, Multiple POV

SETTING: West Texas

PUBLISHER: Indie/Skyhorse Publishing

IN THE VALLEY OF THE SUN

BY ANDY DAVIDSON (2017)

"Only the blood makes us real," she says. "Only the blood."

The fact that this is a debut novel still blows me away. Davidson's storytelling voice is so confident and self-assured. I was drawn to the narrative's smooth pace and natural rhythm. Travis Stillwell is a mysterious young man who is seriously caught up in some bad business. He has a Texas Ranger hunting him down, which I wish I could say is the worst thing hunting him. Unfortunately, something far more dangerous has an eye on him as well. Aimlessly wandering, his travels take him to a barely operating motel run by Annabelle and her young son, Sandy. Something follows Travis there.

Annabelle is now a favorite female protagonist. I immediately fell in love with her quiet spirit and her fierce love for her son. She made so many brave choices. I haven't invested in a character as I did with her in a long, long time.

This story is dark. Pitch-black. It's one of those tales that reaches far back enough into everyone's past so that nobody feels like a villain —and yet, there are villainous acts. There is wickedness. Blood is shed. There are scenes so terrifying that I shudder when I think of a cinematic adaptation . . . but I long for one, too.

There's enough meat on the bones of this story to satisfy any fan of any genre. This isn't just appealing to horror fans—this book would appeal to readers who love the chase between detective and fugitive; the chase between a man and a woman; and, especially, the chase between good and evil.

THE CHILDREN ON THE HILL

BY JENNIFER MCMAHON (2022)

The tragedies we endure shape our lives: we carry them like shadows.

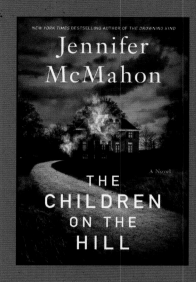

The Children on the Hill is so many things at once—a psychological thriller with a dark mystery at its core and plenty of horror elements. McMahon riffs with a *Frankenstein*-inspired vibe, combining the nostalgia of coming-of-age with the spooky tones of a well-plotted mystery while asking the age-old question: Who is the monster, the creator or the creation?

Dual timelines keep things interesting. The past has a dark, Gothic atmosphere. The present is a fast-paced, suspenseful thriller. Sometimes in a book with back-and-forth timelines, I will favor one or the other, feeling mildly annoyed when the story returns to the one I'm not enjoying as much, but this book kept me invested in both stories.

The timelines are forty or fifty years apart. In the late '70s, Vi and her brother Eric live with their grandmother a stone's throw away from the Hillside Inn, a private mental institution. Helen Hildreth, "Gran," is a prolific psychiatrist who works at the institution. One day she brings home a non-verbal young girl named Iris to stay with them. It's all very mysterious with plenty of clues for readers to gather and savor for later. The three children have an immersive, exciting game they all play together involving classic monsters. Eric is cataloging their "monster hunting" in a book.

The present-day (2019) narrative involves Vi, a grown-up, hosting her podcast, *Monsters Among Us* as "Lizzy Shelley"—a nod to her childhood fascination with monsters and Mary Shelley's *Frankenstein*. She's currently investigating a missing girl who disappeared under mysterious circumstances involving a sighting of a monster. Again, McMahon teases the reader with just enough information to know that there is more to the story than we're currently getting. This keeps the pages turning.

It would be too easy to spoil key plot points—this book has some intricately plotted discoveries. So, the less you know, the better.

AT A GLANCE

THEMES: Orphans, siblings, mental illness, mental institutions, psychiatrists, patients, podcasts, monsters, mysteries, missing people, childhood trauma, child abduction, authors

TONE: Atmospheric, Dark, Eerie, Menacing, Suspenseful

STYLE: Character-Driven, Cinematic, Dual Timeline, Intricately Plotted, Leisurely Paced, Multiple POV

SETTING: Vermont

PUBLISHER: Traditional/Gallery/Scout Press

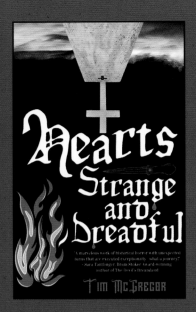

AT A GLANCE

THEMES: Orphans, adoption, family, love, plague, paranoia, superstitions, the occult, witchcraft, evil, unlikely heroes, young adults

TONE: Atmospheric, Eerie, Intensifying Dread, Menacing

STYLE: Character-Driven, Cinematic, Leisurely Paced, Stephen King(ish)

SETTING: New England (1821)

PUBLISHER: Indie/Off Limits Press

HEARTS STRANGE AND DREADFUL

BY TIM MCGREGOR (2021)

Her form seemed to melt through the railing until she was swallowed by the night.

Is it weird to say that a horror book gave me *Little House on the Prairie* vibes while reading it? This had all the atmosphere and nostalgia of my favorite childhood book series, but with hair-raising horror.

Hester Stokely is a capable young orphan who lives with her aunt and uncle, tending to the Stokelys' modest home and farmland in 1821 New England. I can't stress enough how indulgently delicious this book is in its setting and atmosphere. I was fully immersed in this world and invested in the citizens of Wickstead. McGregor does an amazing job of developing characters with meaningful interactions and setting up small-town drama for readers to truly get a sense of authenticity.

The more I felt myself caring for the lives of these fictional people, the more vulnerable I felt to the ominous dread building behind the scenes. What was Tim McGregor going to unleash on these lovely people? At first, it's a disease. Later, it's something far more evil and insidious.

I urge readers to succumb to McGregor's deliberate setup—a sweet, slow burn—and enjoy his carefully plotted story, well-developed characters, and masterful storytelling.

A Creepy Fact!

In mid 1800s Connecticut, the Ray family of Jewett City were sick and dying from tuberculosis. Undiagnosed at the time, the family believed vampires were to blame. In an effort to stop further resurrections, the townspeople began exhuming their loved ones' bodies and setting fire to their decomposing hearts. They even started burying their dead with little bells so that if a corpse tried to dig its way out, the cemetery attendants would hear!

THE RETURN

BY RACHEL HARRISON (2020)

*To love someone is to hate them, a little bit.
We hate everyone we really love.*

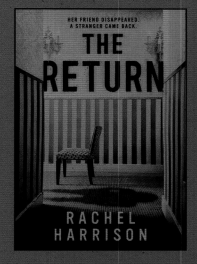

Do we want more female-centric horror? Yes! When do we want it? Now! <Rachel Harrison enters the chat>

The Return is Harrison's debut novel about a tight-knit friend group of women who have seen each other through most of life's major milestones. Julie goes off on a solo hiking trip and never returns. Her closest friend in the group, Elise, never really subscribes to the idea that Julie is gone, even when the other women organize a funeral to celebrate Julie's life.

Eventually, Julie's husband comes home to find Julie sitting on their porch with no memory of how she got there or where she's been. Relieved, the group of friends plan a reunion trip at a quirky, boutique hotel. It's here they start to notice something is off.

This book is a whole vibe about adult friendships and how our early relationships—the ones we developed before fully coming into our own—complicate or hinder our transformation. I was pleasantly surprised by how the storyline splinters into exploring so much more than I anticipated from the book's title. I love Rachel Harrison's brand of horror, and I'll read everything and anything she gives us.

AT A GLANCE

🔍 🔪 GRL PWR

THEMES: Friendship, self-discovery, reunions, missing person, memory loss, strange phenomena, the woods

TONE: Disturbing, Eerie, Humorous, Intensifying Dread, Suspenseful

STYLE: Character-Driven, First-Person POV, Leisurely Paced

SETTING: Catskill Mountains Region, New York

PUBLISHER: Traditional/Berkley

V. Castro

V. Castro's books have captured my whole heart. I feel incredibly lucky to be able to introduce her work to you right now if you have never read any of her books. If you have, let me just say, we are kindred spirits. Castro's brand of horror storytelling typically includes several, if not all, of the following themes: feisty, fiery, spicy, sassy, strong-willed, women protagonists; Mexican American cultural elements, including urban legends, gods and goddesses (mostly goddesses), superstitions, religious practices, family traditions, and social commentary; unique supernatural and paranormal elements; and usually some exploration of sexual tension/light erotica.

In short, her works are unapologetically feminine.

Be smart, but not too smart. Be beautiful, but not so pretty as to make other women mad. Be successful, but not bossy or overly ambitious. Nobody likes a mouthy brown woman. Be a declawed kitten.

If you loved the movie *The Craft*, Castro's *Goddess of Filth* gives me that kind of vibe. A friend group of young, Latina women growing up in Texas and Latin American culture intimately share their unique struggles, hopes, and dreams. One night they're goofing around and accidentally summon an Aztecan entity who embodies their friend Fernanda. The friends watch as Fernanda's whole personality changes and she starts exhibiting strange behavior. Fernanda's mother gets a local church involved, which opens the door to something much more dark and sinister than the ancient power inside Fernanda. *Goddess of the Filth* is a unique twist on possession horror.

In *The Queen of Cicadas*, Castro tells the story of Milagros, a woman working at a farm who finds herself the target of hate. Her dangerous predicament escalates, despite her efforts to flee. In a moment of extreme brutality (that honestly felt like Jesus-symbolism to me), the Aztec goddess of Death, Mictēcacihuātl, supernaturally infuses herself with Milagros' spirit to avenge her murder and exact revenge. Excuse me, but it's fucking awesome. This book is a rush from beginning to end.

In the short story collection *Mestiza Blood*, Castro gives a loud, powerful voice to her heritage and women through stories that reflect the horrors she experienced or witnessed growing up as a Mexican American. There are strong themes of patriarchal oppression, vengeance, justice, revenge, racism, classism, and stereotypes infused into urban legends and folklore. Castro's star is on the rise, and I, for one, could not be happier about that.

RECOMMENDED TITLES

HAIRSPRAY AND SWITCHBLADES (2020)
shapeshifters; paranormal; slasher

GODDESS OF FILTH (2021)
possession; coming-of-age; supernatural

THE QUEEN OF THE CICADAS (2021)
urban legend; vengeful goddess; revenge fantasy

MESTIZA BLOOD (2022)
short story collection

THE HAUNTING OF ALEJANDRA (2023)
folk demon La Llorona; mythology

ALIENS: VASQUEZ (2022)
novelization from the Alien franchise

V. Castro Recommends: "I have been shaped by many frightening stories handed down from my family; however, that young-girl-turned-young-woman had the following books always hissing in the back of her mind. *Scary Stories to Tell in the Dark* by Alvin Schwartz, *Love in Vein* edited by Poppy Z. Brite (I adore everything by him), *Interview with the Vampire* by Anne Rice."

I Grew Up with Ghosts

BY CASSANDRA KHAW

When I was a child, I was told there was a penunggu in every house, and that they weren't the only supernatural entity to roost in a home. There was the Kitchen God too, a garrulous little deity who had to be fed sticky cakes to prevent him from telling the heavens about the household's sins.

And ghosts, of course.

Every kid in Malaysia had a ghost story of their own. Sometimes, it was a personal story. Other times, the tale was a hand-me-down from an older relative, a more adventurous friend. Those who lacked their own often went out to find them. I had friends who would, when time permitted, break into abandoned schools and discarded hospitals to seek sightings of the dead.

None of us were ever really afraid of the supernatural. Wary, sure. Apprehensive, certainly. But not afraid in the way some people are of the dark and the woods and the deep water. It was hard to be terrified of something that felt as natural as the jungles and the monsoon. You only had to be scared when it turned its attention specifically to *you*.

I suspect that is the biggest difference between mainstream Western horror and Eastern horror. With the former, there's often the sense that the good and the everyday is a place untouched by the supernatural—God, of course, being an exception. The hauntings, the possessions, the otherworldly what-have-yous are all anomalous: events catalysed by sin or inattention or interaction with the "exotic." (See: the Indian burial grounds trope.) There is always a cause, and the things that crawl out of the dark are *always* evil.

Eastern horror (and a lot of non-white horror), on the other hand, often posits that we exist side-by-side with whatever else is out there. Rarely is the supernatural malevolent. Sure, it might *kill* our protagonists, might take over their bodies, drive them out of their minds, but it performs such acts with the innocence of a predator animal. It is not corruptive. It is not there to take away souls—not unless requested by a human party. In many cases, these entities would have happily just continued on, ignoring us humans forever, if not for unfortunate circumstances. When that happens, there is nothing to do but to endure, to survive as best we can, and hope we are not altered too thoroughly by the encounter.

I've often wondered about this contrast and how much of it comes from a colonial legacy. Those early settlers, the nervous and seasick explorers, must have told no small amount of stories to each other to domesticate the earth they'd just discovered. They had to be the heroes, the baseline of normal, or none of it would make sense. If they weren't the axis around which the universe rotated, they would have to confront the idea that they were insignificant or worse: intruders parasitizing on lands that did not belong to them, taking away resources that belonged to someone else. That must have been impossible to conjecture when you were trying to convince people that the New World would be the best thing that ever happened to you. (Throw in evangelism and the need to Other and villainize the heathens so you can justify obliterating cultures that were already old when yours was learning to speak, and you have a real recipe for problematic ideologies.)

I wonder as well if this is why mainstream Western horror is so obsessed with naming the bad thing, with giving it a back story, with making tragedy make sense. One of my favourite horror movies is the Pang Brothers' *The Eye*, which features a blind girl who receives a corneal transplant. Following the surgery, she begins to see mysterious apparitions. The film eventually crescendos into a horrific accident and our protagonist being blinded again. The Hollywood remake follows a similar formula, deviating towards the end, with our main characters succeeding in saving at least a few people from their foretold deaths. In the original, the deaths simply happen, the momentum of fate being as inexorable as the elements themselves.

That said, I don't think either storytelling tradition is superior to the other. There is a time and place for everything, a flavor for every individual. Fear, after all, is similarly unique. I'm terrified of goldfish (no, really, I am!) but indifferent to everything else. I have a friend who is inordinately frightened of bears despite never having lived anywhere where bears could realistically be a danger. But horror is certainly more than what Hollywood presents, and I wish sometimes more people were aware of that.

Cassandra Khaw is an award-winning game writer. Their recent novella *Nothing but Blackened Teeth* was a British Fantasy, World Fantasy, Shirley Jackson, and Bram Stoker Award finalist. Their debut collection *Breakable Things* is now out.

SUPERNATURAL

THERE IS A FLAVOR OF supernatural horror for everyone's unique tastes. It's the special ingredient added to a subgenre to level it up to horror status.

Supernatural + Any Subgenre = Seasoned to Perfection

Now, if paranormal horror carries with it that human inclination to have an explanation for strange phenomena, supernatural is the kind of horror that doesn't care about your feelings. This is happening, and there is no reasonable explanation for any of it, so just get on board or you'll lose your mind trying to understand it.

I love how authors will bring that element of human rationality into their storytelling with a character who is stubborn and unwilling to accept whatever horrifying situation they find themselves in. It's relatable. It's also a way for the author to penetrate past the fourth wall and remind us that fiction will require us to suspend our disbelief.

We see this a lot in coming-of-age horror. The young protagonists will experience something so unimaginable that they rush to a caregiver or adult in a position of authority to get help and immediately are met with disbelief. We, the readers, know it's true. We were there when the horrific thing happened to little Johnny, so it's frustrating to know that nobody will believe Johnny and he will be forced to deal with whatever is happening all on his own.

Horror often asks us to quit being the critic. Lay aside that skepticism. Buy into this new reality and completely let go of all of your expectations for how the world should work so that you can enjoy the journey the author has planned for you. This is my favorite way to approach a new book: open to any possibility, ready to invest, available for emotional wreckage and the opportunity for nightmares.

Supernatural horror includes a wide variety of tropes, topics, subjects, and phenomena. Think demons, occult practices, witchcraft, dark magic, cursed objects, scary gods or deities, and on and on into oblivion because of the infinite scope of human imagination. If we can conjure it, storytellers can write about it. This chapter is an endless gift of supernatural horrors that already exist and are waiting to be unleashed upon you.

Demons & Possession

As far as God goes, I am a nonbeliever. Still am. But when it comes to a devil — well, that's something else.

—William Peter Blatty, *The Exorcist*

There are two subgenres of horror that tend to freak me out the most. Demon possession and exorcism make up the first, and cults (page 88) is the other. A religious background or belief in angels and demons is not necessary for demon possession to be scary. It's like the great equalizer of horror, leveling the playing field. This is where atheists and religious folk can hold hands in terror.

I watched the movie *The Exorcist* at a friend's house through my fingers when I was in grade school, and those visuals are seared into my brain. I avoided the book for so long; the trauma nightmares I endured from the movie soured my desire to experience the story all over again.

Several years ago, I finally read *The Exorcist* by William Peter Blatty for the first time. I was like, "I'm Mother-fucking-Horror now. I will read *The Exorcist*."

It scared the bejeezus out of me. I loved it. It was a spiritual experience, igniting my insatiable appetite for demon possession books.

There is something utterly terrifying about the idea that an evil entity can somehow get inside your body and hijack it for its own intents and purposes. The very essence of who we are is attached to our individuality, free will, and personal agency. To have all of that stripped away by a malicious, supernatural being capable of destroying your mind, body, and soul is the stuff of nightmares.

The following books are some of the scariest books I've ever read.

BOYS IN THE VALLEY

BY PHILIP FRACASSI (2023)

Deep down in the darkest parts of his mind, where the evils of the world are caged away for inspection, he finds fresh fear.

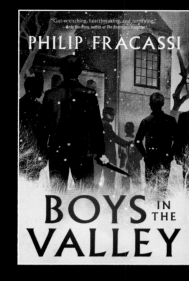

This is the scariest coming-of-age horror I have read since Stephen King's *IT*. It's the scariest demon possession book I've read since *The Exorcist* by William Peter Blatty. Fracassi wrote this book as if it was his mission in life to give horror fans the most satisfying demon possession horror novel ever. Mission accomplished.

Boys in the Valley transports you to a remote location in Pennsylvania, the St. Vincent's Orphanage for Boys. Philip Fracassi masterfully sets the stage for horror by introducing his readers to a cast of boys and young men and the priests responsible for their care.

One night, the peace in the home is disrupted when some men show up with someone badly wounded and screaming. All the commotion wakes up a few of the boys who sneak out of bed to see what is going on. They watch in shock and horror as the afflicted man behaves like a deranged lunatic, his body covered in strange markings. When he dies, the unnatural thing inside this man's body is unleashed upon St. Vincent's orphanage.

Listen. This fucking book.

Boys in the Valley had a limited, exclusive Halloween 2021 release from a boutique publisher. After reading it, there were not very many people I could talk to about it. Well . . . Stephen King saw my tweet about it and responded that he was going to buy it/read it, but that's a story for another time.

It was picked up by Tor Nightfire, and now everyone can find out what I have had bottled up inside me for a few years. This book is original, emotional, and downright terrifying. Some scenes I read with my eyes welling up with tears, and other scenes I read in a state of stone-cold fear. Is this happening? Am I really reading this godforsaken scene? Nothing can prepare you for the full-tilt descent into madness and unadulterated horror Fracassi has in store for his readers. Prepare yourself.

AT A GLANCE

THEMES: Demon possession, young men, orphans, priests, religion, isolation, child abuse, friendship, evil, survival

TONE: Bleak, Blood-Soaked, Dark, Gruesome, Intensifying Dread, Menacing, Shocking

STYLE: Brisk Pacing, Character-Driven, Cinematic, Intricately Plotted, Stephen King(ish)

SETTING: Pennsylvania

PUBLISHER: Traditional/ Tor Nightfire

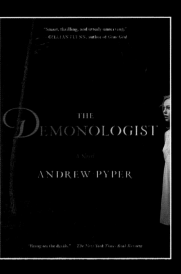

THE DEMONOLOGIST

BY ANDREW PYPER (2013)

"I've never been able to figure out what you're so scared of, but there's something in you that's got you backed into a corner so tight your eyes are closed against it," she says. "You don't have to tell me what it is. I bet you don't even know yourself. But here's the thing: I probably won't be around for you when you face it down. I wish I could be, but I won't. You're going to need someone. You won't make it if you're alone. I don't know of anyone who could."

I could describe the plot of this book for an entire page and would still only scratch the surface. I will let you in on some basics but mostly describe my reading experience because that's what's going to get you to pick this book up.

The basics: Professor David Ullman is an expert on the poem *Paradise Lost* by John Milton. You know, biblical things about Hell, Satan, Adam and Eve, expulsion from the Garden, and all that Genesis origin story stuff. David has suffered a lot of trauma and tragedy in his life. He battles depression, and his marriage is falling apart. A mysterious woman presents David with a strange "quest" of sorts—travel to Italy and lend his expertise to a situation going on there. David brings his daughter, Tess. Things take a very dark turn.

Much like Blatty's *The Exorcist*, this book had a profound spiritual effect on me. I felt it all: characters battling inner demons as well as supernatural ones; going through a crisis of faith; wanting to believe in impossible things, but not being able to commit to the suspension of disbelief; taking that leap; loving people too much; feeling bogged down by darkness or bad thoughts; drowning in anxiety, worry, and grief. David Ullman is the ultimate sympathetic protagonist. I was there with him the whole way through.

Andrew Pyper knows how to take his readers on an inescapable journey rife with personal nightmares. I knew the risk of real terror was high based on how emotionally invested I was. This one lingers.

AT A GLANCE

THEMES: Occult, academics, books, professors, demons, fathers and daughters, marriage, Milton's *Paradise Lost*, skeptics, depression, grief, fear, wandering, faith, hope

TONE: Atmospheric, Bleak, Dark, Eerie, Gruesome, Intensifying Dread, Melancholy, Suspenseful

STYLE: Brisk Pacing, Cinematic, Critically Acclaimed

SETTING: NYC/Italy

PUBLISHER: Traditional/ Simon & Schuster

THE WICKED

BY JAMES NEWMAN (2007)

They stopped building long enough to tilt their heads toward the heavens, and together they sang a dark, unholy song, words not spoken for centuries.

Moloch watched the gathering from his place in Hell, and he said that it was good.

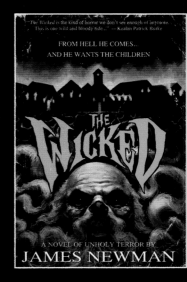

The cover of this book is every indication of the horror and madness *The Wicked* throws down. It is off-the-rails horror, and I loved every single minute of it. James Newman is the kind of author that can plumb the depths of depravity and go completely buck-wild but keep the screws tight on the mechanics to maintain reader investment and deliver on believability.

The characters in this small town are fully fleshed out and likable. Katie and David decide to leave the city and move to a small town in North Carolina to raise their young daughter, Becca. Everything about Morganville is idyllic, even their new address on Honeysuckle Lane sounds too good to be true.

And it is.

An ancient demon was conjured into existence during a horrible tragedy in the town's past. After lying dormant for a season, it's now coming for the souls of the townspeople, especially the children.

This book is full of unadulterated bloody gore and graphic scenes of sex and violence. A very good time. I highly recommend reading *The Wicked* on or around Halloween.

AT A GLANCE

THEMES: Demons, children in peril, moving to the country, small-town horror, a band of survivors, '80s style pulp horror

TONE: Blood-Soaked, Brutal, Disturbing, Gruesome, Intensifying Dread, Shocking, Violent

STYLE: Multiple POV, Vignettes

SETTING: North Carolina

PUBLISHER: Indie/Necessary Evil Press; Apex Book Company (2017)

"A genuinely scary novel about possession and insanity. Hypnotic, disturbing, and written with such unerring confidence you believe every word."
—BRET EASTON ELLIS

COME CLOSER

BY SARA GRAN (2003)

WE COULD devote our lives to making sense of the odd, the inexplicable, the coincidental. But most of us don't, and I didn't either.

This book is terrifying. Maybe because it's a demon possession book, and I find that topic to be extremely unsettling. Or maybe it's because *Come Closer* is just so damn plausible. It's one of the most realistically frightening books in the last twenty years.

Amanda is hearing strange noises and starting to not feel like herself. The more she focuses on these new inconsistencies in her life, the more paranoid she becomes. Ultimately, she believes that she is possessed. Amanda's approach to her situation is so honest and relatable that it's impossible not to see yourself in her situation, which is the scariest thing about this book.

That's what makes *Come Closer* so unique. No two readers are going to engage with it in the same way, and at the end of it, a discussion would prove that there are hundreds of possible conclusions and opinions. This makes it both the perfect book club selection but also a wonderful solitary read because there's nobody to influence all the theories that will begin developing in your mind as you read. Full transparency, it made me feel like I was possessed or vulnerable to demons, which is a sign of great writing. To penetrate past the page and get under the reader's skin like that is a huge testament to the power of immersive storytelling.

THEMES: **Demon possession, marriage, paranormal phenomena, psychological trauma, the female experience**

TONE: **Dark, Disorienting, Disturbing, Eerie, Intensifying Dread, Suspenseful**

STYLE: **Brisk Pacing, First-Person POV**

SETTING: **New York City**

PUBLISHER: **Traditional/ Soho Press**

The Exorcist's Tool Kit

☐ **A CONSECRATED BIBLE:** A SHIELD AGAINST A DEMON'S PERVERSION OF HOLY SCRIPTURES

☐ **HOLY WATER:** SOLEMNLY BLESSED HOLY WATER CAN VEX AN UNRULY DEMON

☐ **A HOLY CRUCIFIX:** PROTECTION; HOLDS A DEMON AT BAY; TERRIFIED OF EVEN THE SIGHT OF IT

☐ **SALT:** BLESSED SALT CAN ACT AS A BARRIER; THE DEMON WON'T CROSS OVER TO HARM THE EXORCIST

☐ **IRON:** USED TO VEX DEMONS

☐ **ROPE:** USED TO BIND THE HOST IF A DEMON IS UNRULY

☐ **ROSARY BEADS:** A SACRED OBJECT USED TO WARD OFF EVIL SPIRITS OR KEEP INTRUSIVE THOUGHTS AWAY

☐ **FAITH:** BEST TO USE THE SIGN OF THE CROSS AND SAY PRAYERS WITH UNWAVERING FAITH

Grady Hendrix

Grady's contribution to horror could be the reason horror is seeing a big resurgence. Now, before the disgruntled murmuring starts about how horror has always been here and readers have always loved it, blah, blah, blah. . .Yes. This is true. But I believe, and this is just one horror fan's opinion, Grady's unique blend of horror, humor, social commentary, and pop culture helped lead the way. Everything about his hit title *Horrorstör* is different. It looks like an IKEA® catalog. It's not a haunted house story, it's a haunted store story. There are illustrations that start as innocuous sketches of furniture but get increasingly more sinister as the story progresses. This book demands attention, and not just from horror fans. People see this clever book and are immediately curious about the content. It's a horror book that reaches across the aisle to welcome newcomers to the genre.

Then *My Best Friend's Exorcism* came on the scene. Another trendsetter, this book is singlehandedly responsible for the popularity of throwback horror. Its paperback cover that everyone had to have with the VHS style artwork. The chapter titles nodding to beloved, classic songs from the '80s. Reading like a heartwarming, endearing love letter to best friends, this book strikes a delicate balance between having enough horror to be terrifying and, yet, still being funny enough for laugh-out-loud moments. It's definitely in my top ten favorite horror books of all time and proves beyond a shadow of a doubt that horror is not just stabby, slashy blood and guts.

And I should mention how Hendrix gave us the gift of *The Southern Book Club's Guide to Slaying Vampires*. Reading standard chick lit is boring to main character Patricia. She yearns for something provocative or scandalous to wake her up from the stupor of the mundane, so her book club starts reading non-fiction true crime books and things get spicier! But then James Harris, a handsome newcomer to the neighborhood, shows up and we go full tilt. This book is so many things at once. It's hilarious, relatable, sultry, sassy, sexy, and scary. (Did you like my spontaneous string of "s" words?)

Photo by Albert Mitchell

RECOMMENDED TITLES

MY BEST FRIEND'S EXORCISM (2016)
demon possession; friendship

WE SOLD OUR SOULS (2018)
metal music; satanic stuff

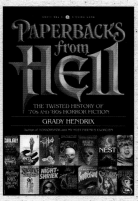

PAPERBACKS FROM HELL: THE TWISTED HISTORY OF THE '70S AND '80S HORROR FICTION (2017)
nonfiction

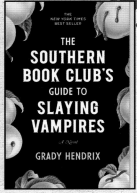

THE SOUTHERN BOOK CLUB'S GUIDE TO SLAYING VAMPIRES (2020)
vampires; women

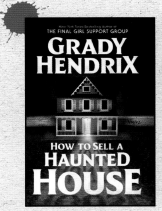

HOW TO SELL A HAUNTED HOUSE (2023)
Haunted house; family drama

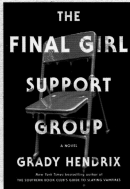

THE FINAL GIRL SUPPORT GROUP (2021)
final girl tropes; slasher

HORRORSTÖR (2014)
haunted store; ghost story

Grady Hendrix Recommends: "Three staggering monuments of horror that don't get read enough are Joan Samson's *The Auctioneer*, which feels like Stephen King's *Needful Things* as written by Cormac McCarthy; Elizabeth Engstrom's *When Darkness Loves Us*, which is a collection of two novellas, one stomach-churning, one heartbreaking; and Bari Wood's *The Tribe*, which might just be the great work of Jewish horror."

The Occult & Witchcraft

Ah, the dark and delicious subject of witchcraft and occult practices. I revel in it. If a new horror release even slightly hints at occult themes or dabbling in witchcraft, I'm drawn to it. My adult persona is mostly made up of all the things that were off-limits or scandalous to me when I was a child, so I'm basically all about sugary breakfast cereals and demonic energy.

My mother told me that ouija boards were portals to hell, so I never touched that shit. If I was at a sleepover and my friends wanted to commune with the dead or have a seance or something, I was out so fast they never even remembered I was there in the first place. Obviously, this is why I like my horror to be steeped in divination and dark magic. I soak up stories about mysterious women living on the outskirts of town rumored to practice witchcraft. Her house is full of bottles and jars, alchemy books, spells, and scrolls. I crave details of ceremonial magic. Immerse me in mysticism. Show me the horrors people face if they mess with a powerful, clever witch. I want to know the spell work involved in cursing one's enemies and the back stories of cunning folk, holistic healers, and midwives.

Horror is often expressed trauma, so horror fiction concerning the occult or witchcraft are typically tales of religious-fueled persecution or oppression on those thought to be practicing paganism. The pagans are the protagonists, the religious organizations represent the antagonists. You will find those stories in my recommendations, as well as the reverse narrative where the witch or occultists are the oppressor. Either way, these tales are seductive and tantalizing.

THE YEAR OF THE WITCHING

BY ALEXIS HENDERSON (2020)

It was the whole of them, the heart of Bethel itself, that made certain every woman who lived behind its gate had only two choices: resignation or ruin.

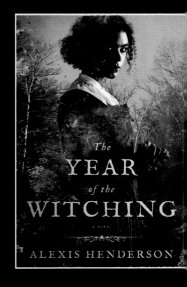

Imagine me stomping around in a circle outside the gates of horror chanting, "We want witches! We want witches!" I mean, as a young girl, I dressed up like a witch or a vampire every year, unless I felt like being Wonder Woman. Witches are quintessential horror icons and there are not nearly enough books about them.

Thank you to Alexis Henderson for giving horror fans a damn good witch story. A young woman, Immanuelle, faces persecution in her puritanical, patriarchal society because she was born of a woman who married and made a family with a man of a different race, was accused of practicing witchcraft, and routinely disappeared into the forbidden forest, Darkwood.

Now Immanuelle finds herself facing the same accusations and assumptions that condemned her mother. A series of plagues descends on Bethel, and Immanuelle might be the only one who can face the darkness. But what Immanuelle discovers is that true darkness is hidden in the hearts of men who pervert the word of God, allowing their lust, power, and desires to run rampant at the cost of the women in their church. Immanuelle must root it out or die trying.

This book stands as a reminder that we have not evolved past the horrors of the Salem witch trials. A warning that society continues to be capable of twisting and perverting religious texts in order to persecute, and ultimately condemn, people who live lives not "approved" by whatever dogmatic leadership is in position of authority.

Some books get a Young Adult (YA) marketing label, and it is appropriate. But some books, like *The Year of the Witching*, get a YA label that's a bit perplexing to me. It's important to make the distinction that not all books with young adult protagonists are intended for a young audience. This one, in particular, will appeal to all ages, so don't let that YA label turn you off. (Note my Pro Tip on page 52.)

AT A GLANCE

😀 🎎 🏛 👤 ⛪ GRL PWR

THEMES: Religion, misogyny, witches, mothers and daughters, patriarchy, race, magic, family secrets, prejudice, secrets, young women, love

TONE: Atmospheric, Disturbing, Intensifying Dread Menacing, Suspenseful

STYLE: Brisk Pacing, Character-Driven, Cinematic, Intricately Plotted

SETTING: N/A

PUBLISHER: Traditional/Ace

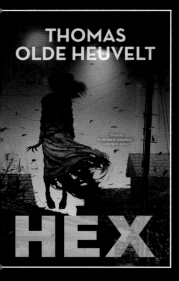

THOMAS OLDE HEUVELT

AT A GLANCE

THEMES: Curses, witch, community, humanity, haunted, quarantine, sacrifice, small towns, social media

TONE: Bleak, Disturbing, Gruesome, Humorous, Menacing

STYLE: Brisk Pacing, Character-Driven, Cinematic

SETTING: Hudson Valley

PUBLISHER: Traditional/Luitingh-Sijthoff (Dutch); Tor Nightfire (English translation, 2021)

HEX

BY THOMAS OLDE HEUVELT (2013)

This is all it takes for people to plunge into insanity: one night alone with themselves and what they fear the most.

Prepare yourself if you read this book at night in your bed. You will turn off the light and imagine a dark shape standing nearby; even with stitches over its eyes, it's still watching you . . . all night long.

Black Springs is an isolated community bound together by a curse. The Black Rock Witch has sealed the fate of every resident of Black Springs—they must accept a life confined to Black Springs and haunted by death. With its stitched-closed mouth and eyes, the witch comes and goes, visiting families at dinnertime or watching the children. The townspeople fear "waking" the witch. Its eyes must always stay closed . . . or else.

This book is about magic and supernatural phenomena as much as it is about human nature. It takes a hard look at our varied responses to fear, which are not exhibited in a vacuum. Trauma responses oftentimes have consequences, harming other people emotionally or physically, or both.

Hex checks so many boxes for me. It's horror with heart: scary, funny, weird, and memorable. I remember exactly where I was while I was reading this book—such a strong experience. It has left its imprint on me, and I hope it will become one of your favorite horror books too.

Pro Tip: Don't Let a YA Label Stop You!

If you're nervous about a YA (young adult) horror book feeling too young for you, look up the book on Goodreads and see how other readers labeled it. If the "Young Adult" label ranks pretty low compared to other labels, it's totally worth your time! For instance, *Clown in a Cornfield* by Adam Cesare had 1,500 readers label it "Horror" and only 400+ labeled it "Young Adult." And that's accurate. It's a great horror book everyone can enjoy.

THE NIGHTMARE GIRL

BY JONATHAN JANZ (2015)

If there is a curse, I believe what we've got is stronger.

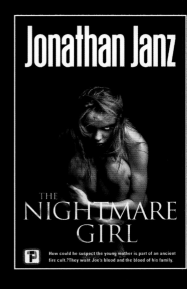

Jonathan Janz has an enormous back catalog of books, so it's tough to know where to start. My favorite books of his are out of print (*Children of the Dark*, *Exorcist Falls*, and *Marla*), so I chose a book that I feel best represents Janz's work that's available on the market right now.

The Nightmare Girl is the story of an average Joe (his name is Joe) who makes an off-the-cuff decision to involve himself in a situation that could potentially change his life forever. Joe Crawford is a stand-up guy. A family man who deeply loves his wife and young daughter. He holds a hard line between right and wrong—even when he's tempted to be drawn in by the allure of something forbidden or to take the easy way out in a difficult situation. Joe is immediately conflicted by his flesh nature, and even though he struggles (because the man isn't perfect), he almost always chooses the "right thing."

Janz does a fantastic job of setting up the story for his readers in the first two parts. His pacing for character building is perfect, so readers can invest in the characters' lives as conflict and tension begin to rise to a boiling point. I could not get enough of Joe Crawford and his "bestie" Darrel Copeland. Their relationship was entertaining and hilarious as they ran around on some amateur sleuthing errands, exchanging witty banter and insults. Joe's relationship with his wife, Michele, is sweet. They're flirty, sincere, and authentic as forty-somethings raising a young girl in a small town.

The antagonists practicing evil witchcraft and the dark, occult themes of this otherwise picturesque story are a stark contrast to the health and vibrancy of the protagonists. It feels realistic. The infiltration of bad people into a well-meaning family. This scenario could easily happen.

I was concerned for my new fictional friends and found myself screaming out against what was sure to be a horrible outcome should situations continue to escalate. The climax and conclusion were BANANAS. There were so many things I didn't see coming, and the ending had me in shambles.

AT A GLANCE

THEMES: Marriage, child abuse, escalation, police procedural, "nice guys"

TONE: Blood-Soaked, Gruesome, Humorous, Melancholy, Shocking, Suspenseful

STYLE: Brisk Pacing, Character-Driven, Cinematic, Intricately Plotted

SETTING: Indiana

PUBLISHER: Indie/Samhain Publishing; Flame Tree Press (2019)

Ania Ahlborn

I'm thankful for Ania Ahlborn and her amazing contribution to the horror genre. Up until I read *Brother*, I labored under the dual illusion that horror fiction was limited to mainstream markets and that there were not very many women writing it. Now I know better. Women have always been here telling terrifying tales worthy of celebration and praise; you just need to know how to find them because they're not always accessible through mainstream markets.

Ania's identifying brand of storytelling is immersive, mesmerizing, suspenseful, and compelling. Her style is character-driven, intricately plotted, briskly paced, disquieting, and haunting. For example, *Brother* is unflinching in its portrayal of a sinister, murderous family that preys on young women, but at the center of all that brutality and carnage is a touching coming-of-age story.

Most of her stories emphasize psychological horror—*The Bird Eater* is one of the most psychological haunted house stories I've read. Readers spend time with Ahlborn's characters who wrestle internally with emotional spiraling: lots of fear, anxiety, worry, doubt, frustration, and anger.

And just look at Ania's impressive back catalog! That's just about one every year since 2011. By the time I discovered her in 2017, she had six books available, each one representing a variety of favorite tropes and subgenres, including an interesting twist on demon possession in her debut novel, *Seed*.

She is now what I have labeled an "Insta-Buy" author. Meaning: Anything she releases, I buy.

RECOMMENDED TITLES

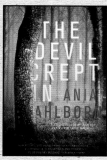

BROTHER (2015)
generational/family horror

THE DEVIL CREPT IN (2017)
missing children; local killer

SEED (2011)
debut novel; demon possession

THE BIRD EATER (2014)
haunted house

WITHIN THESE WALLS (2015)
paranormal; cult horror

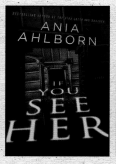

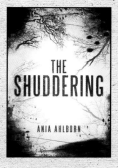

DARK ACROSS THE BAY (2021)
domestic thriller; stalker horror

APART IN THE DARK (2018)
serial killers; ghosts

IF YOU SEE HER (2019)
paranormal; supernatural; small-town horror

THE NEIGHBORS (2012)
bad neighbors; psychological horror

THE SHUDDERING (2013)
scary woods; creature feature; winter horror

Ania Ahlborn Recommends: "If I'm lying in a ravine somewhere, I'm thankful that I read Stephen King's *Misery*, Ira Levin's *Rosemary's Baby*, and William Golding's *Lord of the Flies*. Each offers a unique sort of terror indicative of the darkest parts of our lives."

Cosmic Horror

Cosmic Horror's true terror is best understood as subjugation. A jail
where all hope is a farce and every choice a sham.

—C.S. Humble, author of the Black Wells series

If bleak, nihilistic horror sounds like something you might enjoy, cosmic horror is the subgenre for you. Modern horror authors are forging new paths through cosmic horror, cherry-picking what they love, and infusing it with their brand of storytelling.

I confess to you that I have never read any H. P. Lovecraft, but I also don't feel it's necessary to enjoy the genre. I'm sure there are Lovecraft scholars who would love nothing more than to disagree with me, but life has enough unfair rules and restrictions gatekeeping enjoyment, so in this case, I'm passing out permission slips to go ahead and read whatever the fuck you want.

My invitation to you is this: If you have read H. P. Lovecraft, great. You have an advantage going into modern cosmic horror with all the tenets of the mythos to assist in your comprehension and understanding. You're ahead of the game! If you haven't, here are the bare bones of it:

- Existential nihilism
- Philosophical pessimism
- Natural world/Cosmos desolation
- Cosmic indifference
- Fear of the "other"/the unknown
- Rationality/Sanity
- Malevolent, dark forces and mysterious evils
- Cults
- Secret knowledge, books, texts and chants
- Ancient gods/deities and TENTACLES (a lot of tentacles in cosmic horror)
- Underwater or subterranean beasts/gods

I'm advocating for horror fans to rally around the idea that H. P. Lovecraft established a foundation for cosmic horror, and modern writers of today have erected a whole city on top of it. Anyone can dig down into the footing to explore that foundation, but feel free to skip that part and just appreciate the architecture it inspired. The recommendations I have here are my favorite representations of this subgenre.

THE BALLAD OF BLACK TOM

BY VICTOR LAVALLE (2016)

Nobody ever thinks of himself as a villain, does he? Even monsters hold high opinions of themselves.

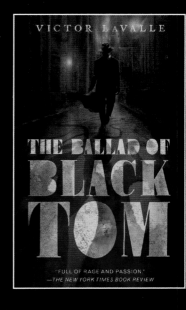

The Ballad of Black Tom deserves to be on everyone's shelves as the gold standard for Lovecraftian fiction, and the source material—"The Horror at Red Hook"—is not required to understand it. LaValle's novella is a response to the racist, antiquated, xenophobic ideologies present in Lovecraft's work by flipping the script. It's an invitation to a new generation of readers to see the imaginative mythos through the eyes of a Black man, a grifter named Tommy Tester. It's genius.

Tommy Tester is making a life for himself in 1920s Harlem by posing as a great jazz/blues musician, even though he's not. He just looks the part. Amidst all his hustling and swindling, he finds himself embroiled with this guy that is bent on some kind of "otherworldly business"; a nameless, threatening fear. At some point, the narrative point of view shifts to an Irish detective, Malone (Lovecraft's narrator), a man in a position of authority who takes a passive role in the racism around him. Admittedly, Tester's narrative is more compelling, but I feel this is by design. This is the perfect introduction to cosmic horror as a whole, and specifically Victor LaValle's work.

AT A GLANCE

THEMES: Social commentary, historical, adaptation, African American culture and experience, racism, magic, science, sons and fathers, immigrants

TONE: Atmospheric, Disturbing, Eerie, Intensifying Dread, Menacing

STYLE: Brisk Pacing, Character-Driven, Cinematic, Multiple POV

SETTING: New York City, prohibition-era

PUBLISHER: Traditional/Tordotcom

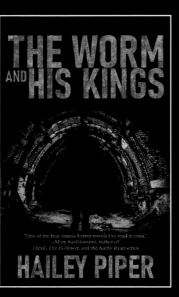

"One of the best cosmic horror novels I've read in eons."
—Mary SanGiovanni, author of
Thrall, The Hollower, and the *Kathy Ryan* series

THE WORM AND HIS KINGS

BY HAILEY PIPER (2020)

"Fear is a symptom. It happens when our old perspective breaks down." Corene stared hard into Monique's eyes. "Sometimes, we have to break down to see things in new ways."

In Hailey Piper's *The Worm and His Kings*, Monique lives on the streets, taking shelter when and where she can. Everything she has in this world has been threatened by the sudden disappearance of her girlfriend, Donna. In a very *Alice in Wonderland* style, Piper leads readers on a journey through a landscape of madness where nothing is as it seems. Monique follows a stranger into a subterranean "wormhole" where she encounters an underground cult and a plethora of creatures—including the one she suspects has taken Donna.

Our "Alice" in this Wonderland, Monique, belongs in my reader's heart forever. Her journey of self-discovery and identity apart from Donna is a gut-wrenching and beautiful tale of transformation. Thrusting the story forward is that age-old power of love, but I adore the way Piper crafted it around a cosmic transcendence. There are Lovecraft influences here, but through the perspective of a uniquely queer lens as it looks at humanity's narcissistic ideology of self-importance. It flips the script entirely since Lovecraft feared the Other, and Piper's cosmic horror centers on the Other.

Prepare for some seriously bone-chilling moments. The ending almost breaks your mind. Keep your eye fixed on Hailey Piper. I expect her career in horror to be in a constant state of rising to the top.

AT A GLANCE

THEMES: Unhoused people, missing loved ones, subterranean society, urban legends, monsters, LBGTQIA+ experience, parallel universes, wormholes, love, humanity, cults

TONE: Dark, Disorienting, Eerie, Intensifying Dread, Melancholy, Menacing

STYLE: Abstract, Character-Driven, Clive Barker(ish), Intricately Plotted

SETTING: New York City (1990)

PUBLISHER: Indie/Off Limits Press

THE FISHERMAN

BY JOHN LANGAN (2016)

My memory relaxed its grip on Marie's death; although it felt more as if her dying loosened its hold on me. The myriad of experiences that had composed our time together became available as more than prompts to grief.

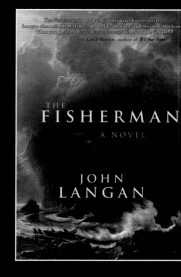

John Langan is one of my favorite authors. Although my love for his work primarily comes from his short fiction collections, his novel, *The Fisherman,* is one of horror's greatest treasures. It features a nested story within a story. Some readers are distracted or let down by that kind of interrupted narrative, but when done well and with a clear purpose, like with *The Fisherman,* I think it can be an effective literary device.

Dan and Abe are acquaintances who are both grieving the death of their wives. They form a relationship around their mutual loss and their love of fishing, which ultimately leads them to a fishing hole of local legend, Dutchman's Creek. The men encounter Der Fisher, who leads them into a great exchange.

Langan's journey promises readers a safe environment to wrestle with one of life's greatest fears: the loss of a significant other. Through the protagonists, Abe and Dan, we observe the natural process of plumbing the depths of grief and the meaning or purpose of life after significant altering circumstances. One man struggles with the oppressive haunting nature of death, while the other can't shake survivor's guilt.

The Fisherman is this great equalizer because every reader is invited to the table to engage with the same story but will experience different outcomes. It sorts people into affinity groups based on varying levels of commitment to the book's resolution. Some will walk away feeling a certain way, while others will describe their feelings in an opposing way, and neither is wrong. It will be interesting to see where you land.

AT A GLANCE

THEMES: Death, friendship, grief, fishing, legends

TONE: Atmospheric, Dark, Eerie, Intensifying Dread, Melancholy, Menacing

STYLE: Cinematic, Critically Acclaimed, Intricately Plotted, Leisurely Paced

SETTING: New York

PUBLISHER: Indie/Word Horde

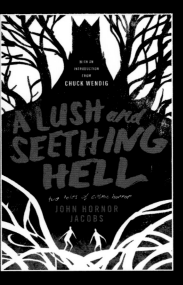

A LUSH AND SEETHING HELL

BY JOHN HORNOR JACOBS (2019)

Violence leaves its mark and horror makes siblings of us all.

This book is made up of two novellas and is responsible for my first bookish jump scare. I read one line and jumped out of my skin just like at the movies.

The first novella, *The Sea Dreams it is the Sky,* is about a poet named Rafael Avendano, also mysteriously known as The Eye, who strikes up a casual friendship with a woman named Isabel. They realize they have a lot in common and their relationship deepens. Jacobs writes with so much attention to detail it's impossible to remember what's unfolding is fiction. I kept reaching for my phone to try and Google "Rafael Avendano" so that I could read more about his life and poetry.

Eventually, Isabel and Rafael's narratives experience a shocking confluence that leaves the reader suspended in mind-reeling bliss. I read one scene over and over again because it was just so powerful. It captured my imagination and led me into a long spell of thoughtfulness, a testament to how thought-provoking horror can be.

Jacobs' second story (and my favorite of the two), *My Heart Struck Sorrow,* is about a librarian weighed down by grief and guilt. He goes on an assignment with a coworker to an estate left in their company's possession by a philanthropist who has passed away. They find a long-forgotten room filled with recordings and journals. I absolutely love stories with found footage and files—it's one of my favorite framing devices.

The narrative then splits between our present-day protagonist immersed in the discovery of these forgotten memoirs and the tale that he's reading about: Two men in the 1930s are commissioned by the Library of Congress to travel around America collecting the songs of the people for posterity. One song, in particular, catches their attention: a murder ballad. This song keeps coming up, and the strange events that happen after it's sung are unnerving. Again, I was captivated by Jacobs' storytelling style and his impressive use of specific details, which really adds to the bone-chilling nature of this story.

AT A GLANCE

THEMES: Cults, research, death, musicians, poets, secrets, oral tradition, librarians, translators, infidelity, obsession, cursed artwork

TONE: Intensifying Dread, Menacing, Suspenseful

STYLE: Cinematic, Critically Acclaimed, Dual Timeline

SETTING: South America (1st story), the South (2nd story)

PUBLISHER: Traditional/ Haper Voyager

WALK THE DARKNESS DOWN

BY JOHN BODEN (2019)

He felt drawn, a bandage being pulled slowly from a wound, marred by pain and suffering but now free to flutter in the air.

Here's a weird, cosmic, adventure, horror, western. If I have to categorize this book by genre, I would say it's something like Stephen King's *The Dark Tower* meets Joe Lansdale's *The Drive-In*.

This story is under two hundred pages, but it still took me days to finish because it's narrated to the hilt. Boden's language is rich and sticky—the words lift off the page for readers to grab ahold of and mull over, meditating on the descriptions, the dialogue, the phrases and sayings. My desire was not to miss anything by reading too fast.

Each chapter follows one (or a combination) of the three protagonists:

JONES: on the hunt for the man who killed his mother. He's pissed off and bristly but finds himself at the home of someone whose friendship is irresistible.

KEATON: a loner who stumbles upon a depressing scene and ends up with a young traveling companion named Jubal

JUBAL: carries with him something alive in a little, makeshift sling

Or it follows our antagonist, Levi. Never before have you read a villain like this. Truly, I had to steel myself for his chapters. Every time I saw a heading with his name, I would take a deep breath.

Levi travels through a western landscape of small, isolated towns leaving a wake of destruction and death. All these wanderers are destined to cross paths at some point.

This is a rare opportunity for readers to fall in love with unlikely heroes engaging in an epic battle against the most formidable enemies you've ever read, both human and cosmic.

AT A GLANCE

THEMES: Child abuse, revenge, killers, evil, traveling, justice, vigilantes, monsters, friendship, love

TONE: Atmospheric, Bleak, Blood-Soaked, Brutal, Dark, Disturbing, Gruesome, Intensifying Dread, Melancholy, Menacing, Shocking, Suspenseful, Violent

STYLE: Character-Driven, Cinematic, Leisurely Paced, Lyrical, Stephen King(ish)

SETTING: N/A

PUBLISHER: Indie/Macabre Ink

Make Horror Gay AF

BY HAILEY PIPER

We horror lovers are a little abnormal, aren't we? Most would say so. Though we each define our preferences within, it's broadly a genre of disquiet, unsettlement, monstrosity, the unknown, and despair.

If that's abnormal, what's that say about normal? We know monsters and despair in life, too. But we feel that pressure of Normal, like brand-name clothing you can't afford. From childhood, we're expected to wear Normal, slice away pieces of ourselves to make it fit, then turn that blade on anyone who won't slice themselves the same way.

When you're an outsider, you go through childhood hearing, "What's wrong with you?" Eventually, you ask yourself that question, too. Why do you feel different? Why are you wrong? Will you ever be able to afford that brand-name Normal? Do you have the desperation to cut yourself into its fit? The ones who've done the cutting can tell. For example, schoolkids knew I was queer long before I did.

Horror fans and queer folk often struggle with brand-name Normal. For me, I saw other queer folk growing up, not knowing I was one of them, sometimes knowing words for them—decent ones as well as the same slurs barked at me—and didn't understand why they were reviled until I realized we were part of that same outsider-ness. None of us fit Normal. Sometimes you understand that means the societal revulsion is unfair and wrong; other times, it's an "explanation" for what's wrong with you.

Horror gets it. We fans know—it's the pariah of genre fiction, the one other genres lock in the attic like a madness-stricken relative in a Gothic tale. Raised eyebrows, shocked faces, questions of "Why do you like that shit?" Even becoming outcasts for alleged devilry.

For all the badmouthing horror gets as depraved or devilish, the genre is a blessing for many.

Certainly we queer folk. Horror has an intrinsic queerness. We are exiles seeing exiles. Sympathy for the devil, empathy for the monster. I remember *Creature from the Black Lagoon* was my favorite as a kid. Poor Gill-man . . . his space invaded in one movie, hauled to a zoo the next, and then his story ends with the leads trying to make him human. They wanted to slice him, make that Normal fit.

I couldn't see it for analogous to conversion therapy when I was little, only knowing what they were doing to the Gill-man was wrong. Monstrous blood is our blood.

There have been attempts to cage horror. Censored books, censored films. It only forces the horror to push through in other directions. We got bloodier. Look at Clive Barker's early works. *The Books of Blood* were a revelation in gore, extremity, sexuality, and yet painted with beauty. In a world shadowed by the Cold War, Reagan, and Thatcher, out came this queer virtuoso unwilling to cut his work to that Normal fit, instead painting in blood: NO.

Barker depicts in *The Hellbound Heart* a paper-thin world of varying facets. Normal is not a default. It is a configuration, one slim layer pretending it's the absolute when there's an ocean of experience to explore.

When I say, "Make horror gay as fuck," my unintentional slogan, it isn't about applying queerness to horror. It's about freeing horror's intrinsic queer beast, the way Barker has, and James Whale, and Caitlín R. Kiernan. Those who see Frankenstein's monster and understand, "Yes, they'd chase us down, too."

That's fiction's freedom. We can find layers outside the Normal, like Roddy Piper's character slipping on revelatory shades in *They Live*. Every story is another layer, another experience, another exploration. Physical and emotional ramifications made manifest, monstrous love stories, the blasphemous possibility for universal change.

Even if it tears the world down.

I was hesitant to grab hold of this abject queerness. My early stories, like my book *The Possession of Natalie Glasgow*, saw timid hints and allusions. But I found readers not only receptive to queer horror, to the mask dropping from the monster—they were ready for it. Our predecessors broke ground, fighting the good fight. Now Carmen Maria Machado, Gretchen Felker-Martin, Eric LaRocca, Aiden Thomas, Suzan Palumbo, myself, and so many more get to be grandiosely queer. Unapologetically queer. Brand-name Normal lashes back, Machado and Felker-Martin know this best, but horror is ready. I tore off any hesitation with *The Worm and His Kings* and *Queen of Teeth*, and I found horror fans eager for fresh voices and stories, new perspectives and explorations. What a welcoming place.

Especially among queer horror fans. We want to see ourselves. Yes, as monsters, we do love them, but we crave the guts of the world, too, the range of horror's truths, triumphs, power, tragedy. With monsters, as monsters, against monsters, against everything, becoming everything. There's an anger here, and a justified one.

But there's also joy. Sometimes it's reading characters like ourselves beset by the creatures we've grown up with, caught between supernatural malevolence and the all-too-human kind. Elsewhere, it's a world painted in our reality. The spectrum of queer experience slides along those layers I keep mentioning, and doesn't Normal seem so tiny against that vastness? Why Normal, when there's thematic transgression, metaphorical transition, or just some queer folk who strayed beneath the wrong eldritch god's star?

Or sometimes, we get to be a righteous scream against a world still trying to fit that brand-name Normal, except the fabric is moth-eaten, and werewolves tear through their clothes at a full moon's transformation.

And damned if queer horror won't see us monsters take the night.

Hailey Piper is the Bram Stoker Award-winning author of *Queen of Teeth*, *No Gods for Drowning*, *A Light Most Hateful*, and other books of dark fiction, as well as over a hundred short stories appearing in *Vastarien*, *Pseudopod*, and other publications. She lives with her wife in Maryland.

HUMAN MONSTERS

Monsters are real, and ghosts are real too.
They live inside us, and sometimes, they win.

—Stephen King

THE STORIES WE TELL about how human beings inflict the worst horrors upon each other are more terrifying than any fictional monster we can imagine. In fact, when I think of the books that have scared me the most in my life, they're usually human monster stories or a combination of the supernatural/paranormal and human monsters. It's hard to choose which is more frightening, the horrors that defy explanation or the monsters who make the headlines of our daily news.

There are monsters in this world. They are capable of incredible evil and despicable acts of violence, and they attack every single day. The monsters we should fear the most are us. Each other. And we don't look like monsters; we look like people you know or sit next to on the bus ride home. They walk right onto our school campuses. They sit waiting inside a parked van in a dimly lit parking lot. There's a monster right now lurking outside someone's house. Stalking. Plotting. Fantasizing.

And that's horror. Real horror. We're all potential victims. We are all capable of doing shitty things to others, and they are capable of doing it too. You might actually be the monster in someone's story. Think about that.

Want More Human Monsters?

I curated an anthology with my Night Worms business partner, Ashley Saywers. It's called *Dark Matter Presents Human Monsters: A Horror Anthology*. This Bram Stoker Award®-nominated anthology includes 35 brand-new human monster stories by many of the authors you can also find on this list of 101 books.

Coming-of-Age

In Greek, "nostalgia" literally means "the pain from an old wound." It's a twinge in your heart, far more powerful than memory alone. This device isn't a spaceship, it's a time machine. It goes backward and forward, it takes us to a place where we ache to go again.

—Don Draper, *Mad Men*

I used to think nostalgia was that warm, fuzzy feeling we get when we're experiencing something we used to love when we were children: the smell of Treat Street at the local carnival, a Christmas parade, an old movie we've watched a hundred times. Recently, my definition has expanded to include the quote above.

Nostalgia isn't just all sweet and good feelings; it's laced with the pain of an old wound. It's a happy memory infused with the knowledge that we can't ever go back there. A bruise that gets pressed, causing a dull ache. And that's why I love it— there is a sweet pain, a hurt that feels good when I read coming-of-age horror.

I enjoy falling in love with a child protagonist with my whole heart and watching them experience growing up into the adult they're going to become. Add horror to this equation and

I'm in my happiest place. Imagine kids on bikes enjoying the summer while saving the world from evil. I can't get enough. This is, hands down, my favorite genre. We can thank Stephen King for this.

Even though we all experienced childhood differently, the fact remains, we were all children once. You and I both have memories of what it was like to be a child. From dependence on the grown-ups in our lives to that sense of wonder and learning as we go, all of our experiences shaped and developed us into the people we are today. As we read horror with child protagonists, we see ourselves. We were defenseless and too curious for our own good in a world made for adults. It's scary out there for kiddos, and the following books I've chosen will take you back to that time in your lives when the world was too big and you were very, very small.

KNOCK KNOCK

BY S. P. MISKOWSKI (2011)

There's no pure good in anybody I've met. People wrestle with themselves and good doesn't always win, even in a person who wants to be good. Wickedness comes looking for a home.

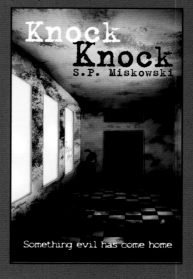

This may be the most underrated book on my list, which makes it one of the most important ones to read. This is a coming-of-age horror centered on the female experience. In a subgenre known for its iconic "boys on bikes fighting evil" trope (*IT*, *December Park*, *Boy's Life*), it's tough to find equally satisfying horror with young girl protagonists. *Knock Knock* is that book.

Our story begins deliciously with three girls who hate the idea of pregnancy and motherhood so much that they agree to sneak off into the woods and perform a ritual to ward off getting pregnant forever. Taking place in a small, fictional town somewhere in the Pacific Northwest, Miskowski tracks the friend group through childhood, adolescent years, and ultimately adulthood.

Each woman's experience is unique to her, shared in a way that feels authentic and relatable. The best part is the underlying sense of dread interwoven throughout the narrative. A growing tension and darkness that ultimately reveals itself pushes the narrative into the most terrifying horror.

AT A GLANCE

GRL PWR

THEMES: Female experience, motherhood, the occult, pregnancy, paranormal, demons, friendship, folk tales, mysticism

TONE: Atmospheric, Dark, Eerie, Intensifying Dread, Menacing

STYLE: Character-Driven, Cinematic, Leisurely Paced, Vignettes

SETTING: Skillute, WA

PUBLISHER: Indie/Self-Published

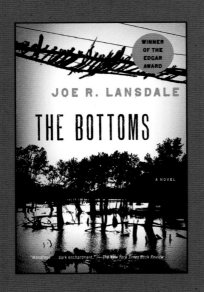

THE BOTTOMS

BY JOE R. LANSDALE (2000)

The sun was starting to shine bright by the time we rolled out of the yard, and while Daddy drove and tried to drink his coffee, I ate my buttered biscuit, and for the first time began to feel that I had stepped over the line of being a child, and into being a man.

AT A GLANCE

THEMES: Fathers and sons, racial tension, murder, injustice, serial killers, family, siblings, kids solving crimes

TONE: Bleak, Dark, Intensifying Dread, Suspenseful

STYLE: Brisk Pacing, Character-Driven, Cinematic, Stephen King(ish)

SETTING: East Texas, the Depression era

PUBLISHER: Indie/Mysterious Press; Vintage Crime/Black Lizard (2010)

This is my big push for Joe R. Lansdale to be a household name. He is an iconic storyteller, not just in the horror genre, but in all genres of fiction. I'm picking the first book I read, and it one hundred percent belongs on a list of the best horror has to offer because if people recommend Robert McCammon's *Boy's Life* or Stephen King's *Joyland*, *The Bottoms* also belongs here. So here it is. Your assignment is to read it because you will never, ever, NEVER forget it.

The Bottoms takes place in East Texas, just after the devastating effects of the Great Depression in the 1930s. Our story zeros in on a family living by a river—an area known as the Bottoms. The father, Jacob Crane (I love this man) is the local constable. He's married to a strong, beautiful woman, and they have two children: Harry, who is around twelve or thirteen, and his sister, Tom (Thomasina) who is just a bit younger.

The narrator is Harry, and he's telling a tale in flashback from a nursing home. I love Harry so much I could cry right now trying to explain how special he is. Lansdale wrote the most endearing and beautiful father-son relationship between Jacob and Harry. In a time when segregation and racial prejudice are at an apex, Jacob teaches his family to treat people fairly, not in a self-righteous preachy way but by leading by example.

Lansdale paints small-town life with exquisite and intimate details. The townies are bright and colorful. I especially loved Miss Maggie and the way she tells stories to young Harry. But this isn't a "feel-good story" of good triumphing over evil all the time—this town is saturated with racial tension and, to add fuel to the fire, there's someone out there murdering prostitutes. Our sweet kiddos Tom and Harry stumble upon one of the first bodies, so their dad Jacob takes up an investigation; a murder mystery that gets more and more intense as the story goes on. This is one of the all-time best coming-of-age horror novels you'll ever read.

DECEMBER PARK

BY RONALD MALFI (2014)

No one referred to the children as dead because none of them were found — not at first, anyway. They were the Missing, the Disappeared. The first few were even thought to be runaways. But all that changed soon enough, and my friends and I were there to see it happen.

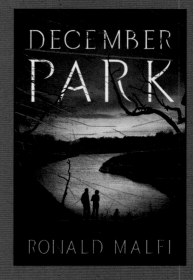

The most enjoyable thing about Malfi's book *December Park* is that the mystery is very slow to unfold (just as I would assume real crime mysteries do). While we're waiting for Malfi to reveal clues pointing to the killer and, ultimately, the killer's identity, we are altogether consumed with the lives of his protagonists: five very different boys around 15 years old who go to high school together.

We spend the most time with Angelo Mazzone. His dad is a police officer working on the case of the "Piper" and the disappearing kids. Angelo makes the case that, while law enforcement must protect and serve, it's the children of Harting Farms that know the underbelly and all the secrets of the town, including the private lives of kids.

Reading about teens during the 1990s is always a treat for me because that was my experience, so I instantly related to the context on a personal level. The music references, slang words, and everything about the setting was striking a chord. My favorite scenes were whenever all of the boys were together for pages of dialogue—it's like you're right there as a fly on the wall witnessing real boys in the summer of their youth. All of their struggles, joys, attitudes, emotions are expressed realistically by an author who lived it and can pull from a deep well of knowledge and experience.

I always say that the best horror books are the ones where the reader falls in love with the characters because the risk becomes so high when our lovable characters are faced with danger. This book is no exception. By the end, I was wrecked, and I loved every moment of feeling those feelings.

AT A GLANCE

THEMES: Childhood, friends, school, serial killer, teenage boys, child murder victims

TONE: Dark, Disturbing, Gruesome, Humorous, Intensifying Dread, Menacing, Suspenseful

STYLE: Character-Driven, Cinematic, Intricately Plotted, Leisurely Paced, Stephen King(ish)

SETTING: Maryland (the 1990s)

PUBLISHER: Traditional/ Medallion Press; Open Road Media (2021)

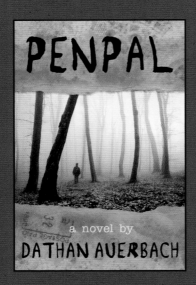

PENPAL

BY DATHAN AUERBACH (2012)

*As children we have terrific and terrible times —
events that, as we experience them, seem to be the
most important things that have ever happened to us —
but more often than not we forget them. Truth to tell, at
any point in our lives we've forgotten more than
we know about our own history.*

AT A GLANCE

THEMES: Childhood, memories, school, the woods, parents, stalkers, pen pal, friendship, missing child

TONE: Disorienting, Eerie, Melancholy, Menacing, Suspenseful

STYLE: Abstract, Brisk Pacing, Vignettes

SETTING: N/A

PUBLISHER: Indie/Self-Published

There is nothing traditional or standard about the book *Penpal*. It started as short, interconnected stories posted anonymously on the "No Sleep" Reddit forum. The popularity of the stories spread like wildfire, ultimately leading the author, Dathan Auerbach, to come out of anonymity and publish the stories as a book: *Penpal*.

By the time I caught wind of the book, reader reviews were fairly polarizing. It seemed to me that people either "got it" and loved it or were left disappointed by the hype. I love finding horror books that are simultaneously so loved and hated. It's exciting to see which side of the fence I'll land on. I hope other readers feel the same way. A bookish challenge!

Since this book is on my 101 list, you know that I'm on Team *Penpal*. I think it's brilliant.

The horror is offered through a realistic account of the narrator's strange childhood experiences. The memories are disjointed snippets of events cobbled together to create a larger picture of something potentially very sinister.

This is one of those books that every reader will engage with differently depending on their preconceived notions of what is believable and what might be too far-fetched. For me, the simplicity and straightforward delivery stuck the landing.

I'm partial to coming-of-age horror anyway, and I have an appreciation for human monsters, as opposed to supernatural or paranormal ones. Whether you love this one or hate it, its origin story and unique format stand out in the genre.

OF FOSTER HOMES AND FLIES

BY CHAD LUTZKE (2016)

I've seen plenty of movies where police investigators cower in disgust at the scent of a rotting body, covering their mouths, struggling to hold down their lunch. But all the Hollywood reactions in the world couldn't have prepared me for the real thing.

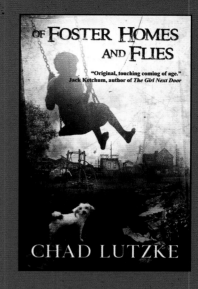

This is where I'm going to challenge your definition of horror and what does or doesn't belong in the genre. Horror is a spectrum.

Of Foster Homes and Flies is about a young boy named Denny who fends for himself for the most part. His mother is usually parked in front of the TV, and one day Denny discovers she's dead.

He goes about his normal activities because he's unsure of what to do and what will happen to him if he calls the authorities. The possible disruption might mean he won't get to compete in the school's spelling bee, which is what his dear, young heart wants more than anything. So, he lives in his home with the corpse of his dead mother.

That's horror.

It's summertime in New Orleans. Our young Denny has to sleep at night with a rotting corpse in the living room deteriorating at an alarming rate in the heat.

Nothing is jumping out of closets, and his mother isn't resurrected, but there is something hauntingly beautiful about this tale, and it deserves to be in everyone's library.

Chad Lutzke's storytelling style is as accessible as it is heartwarming. It's not fussy or flowery with purple prose. It shoots straight from the hip and reminds me of Joe Lansdale's signature, lean style. The definition of horror with heart.

AT A GLANCE

THEMES: Young boys, mothers, neglect, grade school, spelling bee, first love, summer

TONE: Eerie, Gruesome, Humorous, Melancholy, Menacing

STYLE: Character-Driven, Cinematic

SETTING: New Orleans

PUBLISHER: Indie/Self-Published

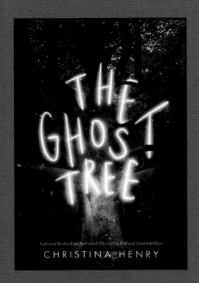

National Bestselling Author of *The Girl in Red and Looking Glass*

CHRISTINA HENRY

THE GHOST TREE

BY CHRISTINA HENRY (2020)

Because we are a branch of the same tree that made those witches long ago.

I lived for this book while I was reading it; it gave me intense *My So-Called Life* vibes, if you've ever seen that show with Claire Danes and Jared Leto. If you haven't seen it, think high school, teenage, female friendships centered around small-town drama, boys, and coming-of-age themes, but toss in a murder mystery.

Christina Henry entices readers to travel back in time to the 1980s to a small town called Smith's Hollow. We follow best friends Lauren and Miranda, their longtime friendship suddenly hitting that "drifting apart" stage. Miranda is looking to make friends with older boys who drive, while Lauren resents being dragged along as a third wheel.

Wrapped in this compelling small-town drama is something more insidious than teenage boys. Two girls Lauren's age are found murdered, their bodies mutilated, in the backyard of one of her neighbors. Miranda couldn't care less and is more interested in finally losing her virginity, but Lauren is plagued by visions that seem related to the murders. She is determined to solve the mystery of the dead girls, especially since she lost her father to violence just two years prior.

I loved this book. The atmosphere was carried through the entire story and left me feeling very satisfied at the end. Quintessential reading for coming-of-age horror told through a female gaze.

AT A GLANCE

THEMES: Teenage girls, murder, creepy woods, supernatural, carnivals, friendships, dating

TONE: Eerie, Intensifying Dread

STYLE: Character-Driven, Intricately Plotted, Multiple POV

SETTING: Small-town USA

PUBLISHER: Traditional/Berkley Books

THE DEER KINGS

BY WENDY WAGNER (2021)

The phone went silent. Gary kept its warmth pressed to his ear another minute, as if he could absorb just a little more of his big sister's comforting presence through the line. As if she could keep him from thinking about the fog, and Calhoun Lake Road, and the summer before his parents stopped being themselves.

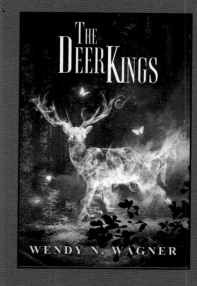

This book is especially for anyone who grew up in a small, rural town that emphasized high school football more than the arts. I see those hands. There are a lot of us. Now let me see the hands of readers who enjoy folk horror. Coming-of-age stories with protagonists you get emotionally invested in? I see you. My Stephen King Constant Readers, this book is for you.

A ragtag friend group of outcasts in rural Oregon summon a god in the woods to protect themselves from a common enemy. Years later, they discover their "Deer Saint" is still active and growing stronger. So not only do the protagonists face supernatural monsters, but also human ones.

The novel toggles between the past and future narratives. My favorite aspect of this book is that it feels heavily inspired by Stephen King's *IT*, but the kids, the "Losers Club" if you will, reflect the more updated teen issues of the 1990s (which was when I was in high school, class of 1994): single parents, drug abuse, poverty, homophobia, and racism.

I love horror with the kids-on-bikes trope and a fierce fellowship of misfit vibes, and this book has it in spades. Later, when the kids are grown and have to come together in a new fight to save their town, Wagner explores the tension of a childhood bond that does not quite meet the expectations of adulthood. Something I think we can all relate to—drifting apart from the people who were everything to you when you were younger.

Some serious horror mixed with the nostalgia of youth, this book is a hell of a good time.

AT A GLANCE

THEMES: Childhood, child abuse/neglect, drug use, homophobia, queer kids, racism, child sexual assault, gore, death, small town, football, high school

TONE: Dark, Disturbing, Gruesome, Humorous, Intensifying Dread

STYLE: Character-Driven, Cinematic, Dual Timelines, Leisurely Paced, Stephen King(ish)

SETTING: Oregon

PUBLISHER: Indie/JournalStone

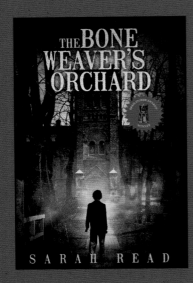

THE BONE WEAVER'S ORCHARD

BY SARAH READ (2019)

In the darkness, he felt the heaviness of stone all around him like a tomb. He felt the hollowness of the long halls, cold as a lost knife and dark as a throat.

Get ready to fall in love with the main protagonist, Charley Winslow. This young man is so sweet and eccentric with his little passion for insects. He's brave and curious. He's left on the front steps of a dark, intimidating boarding school called The Old Cross School for Boys. The attendant who answers the door tries to turn him away, but ultimately realizes he has nowhere to go and invites him in.

Charley gets settled and learns that something prowls the halls at The Old Cross and boys mysteriously go missing.

The staff always says that the missing boys ran away. Of course, Charley, being the curious young boy that he is, witnesses a shadowy figure in his dorm room one night. He also discovers something alarming when he follows some insects into a hidden space in the wall. Strange things are happening, and Charley is not one to focus on his studies nor ignore the potential to find out why boys keep disappearing.

This is one of those books that horror fans devour in one sitting. The Gothic atmosphere is immediately immersive. Read's prose is a feast!

Even though the main protagonist is a child and dark academia typically lends itself to a more Young Adult vibe, *The Bone Weaver's Orchard* is intended for readers of all ages. For me, this book delivers on so many horror expectations: fascinating characters, an opportunity to invest in their fictional lives, suspense, horror, and full engagement in a compelling plot that never lulls. This is easily one of my favorite books.

AT A GLANCE

THEMES: A boarding school for boys, orphans, bug collecting, missing children, murder, buried secrets

TONE: Atmospheric, Dark, Intensifying Dread, Melancholy, Menacing, Suspenseful

STYLE: Character-Driven, Cinematic, Intricately Plotted

SETTING: 1920s England

PUBLISHER: Indie/JournalStone

THE LISTENER

BY ROBERT MCCAMMON (2018)

What I'm sayin' is . . . life is so full of mysteries that only the Good Father can answer. We can't pierce the veil. I don't know how I do what I do. It's grown on me is all I can say.

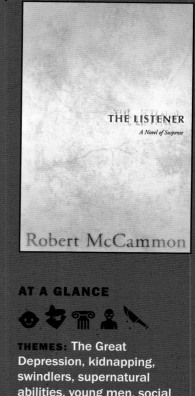

THE LISTENER
A Novel of Suspense

Robert McCammon

The Listener is a great gateway into Robert McCammon's work. A genre mash-up of supernatural suspense, historical fiction, crime drama, and coming-of-age.

Set in 1934, this story is told in parts. First, we are introduced to the immoral, unscrupulous adults John Parr/Pearly and Ginger LaFrance, who swindle folks to make their way during the Great Depression. McCammon scandalizes us with what some people are willing to do to survive. This kind of evil knows no bounds.

In contrast is the story of our main protagonist, Curtis Mayhew, a young Black man who lives with his spirited mother, Orchid, and works at a train yard helping weary travelers with their luggage and such. An honest living.

I was blown away at how effortlessly McCammon transported me to the setting of his story. I could see it all through Curtis' eyes. Every situation he found himself in was just another way for McCammon to reveal more layers of this young man's character. I fell in love with him.

Later, we meet Nilla—a girl about the same age as Curtis but born into privilege. Soon, it is revealed that Curtis and Nilla are unique, and it's their shared characteristic that will bring them together.

The lives of all these characters intersect under some very intense circumstances, and I'd say the last 200 pages MUST be read in one fell swoop. You won't be able to put this book down once the story climaxes and begins its push toward the finish. I never wanted it to end. The last line of this book damn near broke my heart in two. Okay, I think it did.

AT A GLANCE

THEMES: The Great Depression, kidnapping, swindlers, supernatural abilities, young men, social commentary, heroes, self-sacrifice, kids in peril, classism

TONE: Intensifying Dread, Suspenseful

STYLE: Character-Driven, Cinematic, Intricately Plotted, Stephen King(ish)

SETTING: New Orleans, Louisiana

PUBLISHER: Indie/Cemetery Dance Publications

Josh Malerman

I brought *Bird Box* with me on a little anniversary camping trip to the North Coast. I wish I could properly tell you how atmospheric it was to read this story about a woman going through the early stages of an apocalyptic event while I was all snuggled up in a camper by the sea. I became an instant Malerman fan on that trip.

Malerman's storytelling style is fearless when it comes to letting the imagination run wild and unrestrained. I get a real sense that he doesn't hold anything back from the page; he's willing to try anything and isn't too concerned with following trends or maintaining a specific brand. *A House at the Bottom of a Lake* is this summer love story about two teens that find a little boat, a secret lake, and a house underwater. It's eerie and magical. Totally unlike *Bird Box* in every way. Just this secret space for readers to slip into and experience this whole mixed bag of emotions.

I'm certain this is what his fanbase loves the most about his work—expecting the unexpected. *Pearl* is like Malerman's take on *Cujo*. A big, scary pig on a farm with some kind of telekinetic power of suggestion so strong and so evil, the people around Pearl are unsafe. It's downright horrifying in the best possible ways. I mean, an evil pig. Who would have thought?

It's important to note that Josh Malerman is also a musician. He's in a band called The High Strung (they did the theme song for the hit TV show *Shameless*). Did I mention he's involved in movies too? In the movie production industry with his friend and business partner, Ryan Lewis, their company Spin a Black Yarn produced *We Need to Do Something* (page 137)—a horror movie based on a novella by Max Booth III. A real renaissance man shaping the genre from multiple disciplines, Malerman tells stories in three ways: books, music, and movies.

Photo by Darrel Ellis

101 HORROR BOOKS TO READ BEFORE YOU'RE MURDERED

RECOMMENDED TITLES

BIRD BOX (2014)
*apocalyptic survival;
creature feature*

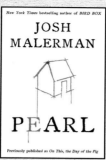

PEARL (2021)
evil animal

MALORIE (2020)
*sequel to Bird Box;
apocalyptic survival*

**A HOUSE AT THE
BOTTOM OF A LAKE
(2021)**
romance; coming-of-age

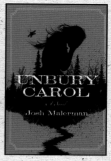

**UNBURY CAROL
(2018)**
weird western; revenge

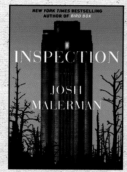

INSPECTION (2019)
*dark academia; human
monsters*

**BLACK MAD WHEEL
(2017)**
weird phenomena; sci-fi

GOBLIN (2021)
*six connected novellas in
the town of Goblin*

DAPHNE (2022)
*Bram Stoker Award®-
nominated; urban legend;
haunting; slasher*

Josh Malerman Recommends: "A trio of books someone would have to pry off my bookshelf are *Strangers on a Train* by Patricia Highsmith for its premise, *Perfume* by Patrick Süskind for its prose, and *The Exorcist* by William Peter Blatty for setting the scariest table I've ever sat at."

Grief, Loss & Death

And the most terrifying question of all may be just how
much horror the human mind can stand and still maintain
a wakeful, staring, unrelenting sanity.

—Stephen King, *Pet Sematary*

Most of the horror authors I have interviewed or talked to over the years have said that the thing that scares them the most is losing a loved one or watching them suffer through something awful. The C-word specifically–cancer–terrifies me. I feel like in some form or another, it comes for us all. There's that impending sense of doom looming in the back of my mind sometimes, especially when I'm reading a book or watching a movie with a main character who has a terminal illness. I can't help but think of myself or my loved ones as my mind floods with that overwhelming sense of helplessness. The tragedy of suffering.

These are such big feelings, and we all wrestle with them. The comfort of reading about it in horror fiction is that it's a safe, welcoming place for me to engage in these thoughts from a distance. I can invest in the characters, fall in love with them even, and then allow my empathy to run wild with the storyline. I give permission to the author to enter those secret places of my heart that don't get shared with others and tap into those fears. It's a communal way of exchanging our fears and anxieties about grief, loss, and death without the risk of actually going through tragedy. Or for people with such experiences, it's a way to relate.

Horror is cathartic and healing in ways that other genres can't even come close to being. The books in this section are an emotional rollercoaster designed to exercise your gifts of empathy and compassion.

RED

BY JACK KETCHUM (1995)

There were so many hidden realities in the world, so many secret lives. It seemed like nobody lived just one.

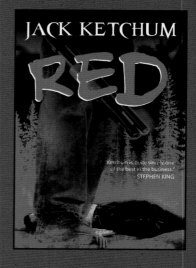

This is the oldest book on the list, but that's because I'm trying to save your soul right now. You're welcome.

Stick around in horror long enough and you're going to start hearing the name Jack Ketchum. And these people are going to tell you *The Girl Next Door* by Jack Ketchum is one of the best, scariest horror books they've ever read. It's going to show up in a lot of recommendations and eventually, despite the warnings, you will buy it and read it and it will scar your very soul.

I wish I could go back in time and ask which Jack Ketchum book I should have read instead of *The Girl Next Door*. And that's why you're lucky because I'm going to do you the favor of suggesting *Red*. Skip *The Girl Next Door* and reach for *Red*.

This one is difficult too because there is a brief scene of senseless, animal cruelty right in the beginning. That's not a spoiler. This act of violence is the catalyst for the rest of the book. In perfect, masterful storytelling, the reader is a witness to a horrific crime committed against a man and his furry best friend.

But Avery Ludlow isn't going to let it go.

Based on the very short synopsis, I was unprepared for how much emotional investment would be required of me. With all the accolades Ketchum gets for being the scariest and most extreme horror writer, his best skill—writing characters readers fall in love with—is severely downplayed. Which leads me to believe that is why his books are so widely discussed and polarizing. Some people want their horror with a certain level of emotional detachment. It makes it easier when the body count keeps rising. If you care about the people enduring hardship and suffering at the hands of impossible evil, the risk is so much higher. Reading hurts your heart!

And this one does hurt, but the feelings are rich. Worth it.

AT A GLANCE

THEMES: Revenge, justice, senseless violence, animal cruelty, man's best friend, badass old men, corrupt suburban aristocracy

TONE: Bleak, Brutal, Gruesome, Melancholy, Shocking, Suspenseful, Violent

STYLE: Brisk Pacing, Character-Driven, Cinematic, Stephen King(ish)

SETTING: Maine

PUBLISHER: Traditional/ Headline Book Publishing (U.K. edition); Leisure Books (U.S. edition, 2002)

I'M THINKING OF ENDING THINGS

BY IAIN REID (2016)

Just tell your story. Pretty much all memory is fiction and heavily edited. So just keep going.

AT A GLANCE

THEMES: Relationships, self, snowed-in, family dynamics, dinner with the parents, secrets, identity, car travel, feeling trapped

TONE: Disorienting, Eerie, Intensifying Dread, Melancholy

STYLE: Abstract, Character-Driven, First-Person POV, Intricately Plotted

SETTING: Intentionally ambiguous

PUBLISHER: Traditional/ Gallery/Scout Press

This book is like nothing I have read before and nothing I will ever read in the future. I had no idea how to categorize it, so this will have to do. It's an enigma. I don't believe anyone will ever say, "Oh yeah, that book reminds me of *I'm Thinking of Ending Things*." Nothing will remind you of this book. It stands alone, all by itself as its own thing and that's why it's important to read it.

I had trouble pulling a quote that would capture the essence of the story because literally everything could have been a great quote to feature. The main, nameless character spends all this time in her head while she's in the passenger seat of her partner's car driving to his parent's house to have dinner. All of these thoughts she's having are so introspective and provocative. It's mesmerizing.

It gets in your head. There is this unnerving feeling that there is a lot of subtext going on just under the surface of what you're reading, but you, the reader, can't get to it. The author has hidden it from you.

There are certain reveals in the story where you think you've pulled a thread out to follow—a little theory to cling to—but those threads are quickly pulled away as the author leads you somewhere else. After a very odd dinner, the couple gets back in the car to head home, making a few detours. That's all that can be said. Don't go into this book with any expectations or preferences. It's not as enjoyable if you don't surrender to the author and allow him to lead the experience. I've noticed that readers who give unfavorable reviews were working way too hard to figure things out and honestly, that kind of mental exercise will spoil your experience. Just let go.

You are totally on your own as far as I'm concerned, and it is my opinion that you should buy this book before someone spoils everything for you and read it straight through in one sitting.

Then, follow the author's instructions when you're done. You'll see.

RED X

BY DAVID DEMCHUK (2021)

You create a thing and you think you can control it, but sometimes it turns on you, it starts to control you. It knows your weaknesses because you made it, it's part of you. It can reach right into you.

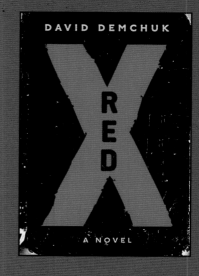

I couldn't decide if I should put this book on the list or Demchuk's Romanian folklore horror *The Bone Mother*. Ultimately, I chose *Red X* for its important contribution to LBGTQIA+ representation in horror. Both *Red X* and Demchuk's first novel, *The Bone Mother*, tell essential stories from marginalized people threatened by suppression and persecution.

To set early expectations, *Red X* is what I would call fictionalized realism in that it is loosely based on real-life horrors that took place in Toronto's Gay Village. There are fears felt by being "other" in a society that doesn't protect or even respect marginalized communities, especially while gay men are being actively targeted by a predator and authorities don't seem to care.

The book begins with a young man named Ryan going missing. There's all this speculation and mystery surrounding his disappearance, but he was new to the community and not very well-known. This is in the '80s, so the internet wasn't even a thing—he just vanishes. Later, other men suffer the same mysterious fate. The thread that connects them all is just not being "seen" by the people around them; nobody misses them or advocates for their safety.

It's also metafiction—the author peppers the fictional story with his own personal experiences growing up gay, social commentary, and thoughts on gay horror fiction. It's on this list because it provides insight and clarity into the very real terror queer people face every day and how society's inclusion and protection offered through community and strength in numbers is the only real way to help offset or eliminate those fears.

It is truly horrifying and, frankly, difficult to experience. My reading journey was that of immense concern, a heavy feeling of dread and anxiety, as well as this growing sense of urgency to check on my queer friends and family to make sure they're not suffering from the neglect communicated in this book.

AT A GLANCE

THEMES: Homophobia, AIDS/HIV, missing persons, oppression, serial killers, the "other" experience, community

TONE: Dark, Disturbing, Gruesome, Intensifying Dread, Melancholy, Menacing, Shocking

STYLE: Abstract, First-Person POV, Leisurely Paced

SETTING: Toronto, Canada (1980s)

PUBLISHER: Traditional/ Strange Light

RITES OF EXTINCTION

BY MATT SERAFINI (2019)

This is desperation. And desperation breeds sacrifice.

Nothing is more terrifying than the idea of losing a loved one to an act of violence. I've stood at the edge of thinking about such things and peered down into the abyss—the utter ruin and darkness of a painful tragedy. It could break me wide open. I don't know how to survive that if I'm honest.

This story follows Rebecca Daniels, a private investigator who has abandoned a normal life so she can devote herself to hunting down her daughter's killer.

The author does an excellent job of slowly unpacking the circumstances of the murder of Rebecca's daughter throughout the book. Investigating this case has become her therapy, her coping mechanism instead of processing grief.

The protagonist has tunnel vision, only seeing revenge as the ultimate solution for relieving the pain and suffering she's going through. It's gut-wrenching to watch the character trainwreck her relationships and well-being to pursue the means to an end—which, in her mind, is her only tangible plan for healing.

However, this isn't just a revenge story. The people that Rebecca encounters bring her closer to knowing what happened, but this knowledge comes at a price.

Rites of Extinction is as dark and disturbing as it gets. It's amazing to me how Matt Serafini managed to bring something original and unexpected to this novella. I've never read anything quite like it. I would also hedge a bet that not one reader will see the ending coming. It took me completely by surprise—there were absolutely no breadcrumbs or clues along the way that would hint at what was to come. If there were clues, and I'm mistaken, then I missed them because Serafini holds his cards close to the vest. This book brilliantly delves into a broken psyche with the page-turning energy of a murder mystery and the distinctive elements of horror dogging the reader the whole time.

AT A GLANCE

THEMES: Obsession, revenge, grief, alcoholism, private investigation, vigilante justice, mothers and daughters, sacrifice

TONE: Blood-Soaked, Disturbing, Intensifying Dread, Melancholy, Menacing, Shocking

STYLE: Brisk Pacing, Character-Driven, Cinematic, Intricately Plotted

SETTING: New Hampshire

PUBLISHER: Indie/Grindhouse Press

FULL IMMERSION

BY GEMMA AMOR (2022)

I found my body early on a Tuesday.

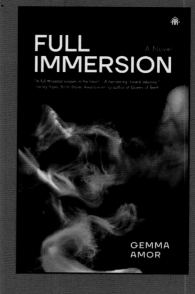

It's my personal opinion that women are overqualified to write horror. The female experience in this world comes with built-in potential for horror. Tune in to any recent episode of any true-crime podcast or TV show, and listen to the 101 ways women are victimized every single day. Or listen to a woman tell their birthing story.

In a world where everything tries to kill us, women survive.

In Gemma Amor's *Full Immersion*, the protagonist, Magpie, is suffering from amnesia and other psychological trauma when she discovers her own corpse by a river. She doesn't have any memory of contacting a medical institution for help during a mental health crisis. Readers know that the institution is monitoring her vitals in a medical lab while her brain is under simulation as we're watching her try to solve the mystery of her death.

This is horror as therapy in its most raw, vulnerable form.

The author shares in the foreword that Magpie's story was inspired by her battle with postpartum depression and advocating for her mental health.

This story impressed upon me the importance of personal agency, the value of our lives to ourselves (and to the people who we love), and the immutable power of storytelling. Gemma Amor shares with her audience that writing this book saved her life. I'm willing to bet that readers will go on this journey with Amor, see themselves in the protagonist, and confess that the hope shining brightly through the darkness saved their lives too. Or at least it will set them on the road to recovery by encouraging them to reach out for help and advocate for themselves.

The beauty of horror, in all its forms, never ceases to amaze me.

AT A GLANCE

THEMES: Suicidal ideation, intrusive thoughts, postpartum depression, traumatic childbirth, implied harm to a child, medical institutions, virtual reality

TONE: Dark, Disorienting, Disturbing, Melancholy, Shocking

STYLE: Abstract, Character-Driven, Cinematic, Intricately Plotted, Multiple POV

SETTING: Bristol, England

PUBLISHER: Traditional/Angry Robot

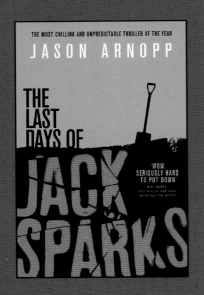

THE LAST DAYS OF JACK SPARKS

BY JASON ARNOPP (2016)

How I wish Jack had never attended that exorcism.

How I wish Jack had never laid eyes on that YouTube video.

Rest in Peace, my brother, and please know that I forgive you.

AT A GLANCE

THEMES: Consequences, death, exorcism, demon possession, ghosts, investigative journalism, YouTube and YouTube sensations, fandom, skepticism, found footage, brothers, karma

TONE: Eerie, Humorous, Menacing, Suspenseful

STYLE: Brisk Pacing, Character-Driven, First-Person POV, Intricately Plotted, Multiple POV

SETTING: Travel/Multiple Locations

PUBLISHER: Traditional/Orbit Books

This is the book I refer to whenever people claim that protagonists have to be likable for the book to be enjoyable. The main character, Jack Sparks, is many things, but above all else, he's a narcissistic, egotistical asshole. What kind of jerk goes to a church in a foreign country and then laughs out loud during an exorcism? This guy!

Jack Sparks reminds me of those internet sensations with millions of followers on YouTube. Their monetized video content funds a lavish lifestyle of video gaming, humble-bragging, and staged, performance-based stunts like "exploring Suicide Forest" or pulling dangerous, nonconsensual pranks on unsuspecting people.

The formatting of this book is extremely experimental and relies on readers engaging with it differently than they would a traditionally narrated, linear story. It's formatted as a manuscript that Jack wrote while researching the occult for his new book, only it remains unfinished because he died. As Jack's brother reads through it, making notes, it becomes tragically clear that Jack was obsessed with maintaining his online persona much to the detriment of his real-life relationships.

Jason Arnopp leans into the crazy world of social media personas, and all manner of technology, showing how it's the best and worst thing humanity has ever created. There are not enough found-footage horror books out there, so I treasure this one and recommend it all the time, especially to people who love Grady Hendrix (page 48), because this one is perfectly hilarious and scary at the same time.

For how utterly ridiculous Jack Sparks is, and for how laugh-out-loud funny the story is at times, I spent most of my reading experience genuinely freaked out.

Queens of Horror

There are some undisputed reigning Queens of Horror. Their names are synonymous with their supreme contributions to the horror fiction industry. Allow me to introduce them.

MARY SANGIOVANNI: THE QUEEN OF COSMIC HORROR

NUZO ONOH: THE QUEEN OF AFRICAN HORROR

GEMMA FILES: THE QUEEN OF HORROR CULTURE

BEVERLEY LEE: THE QUEEN OF VAMPIRES

LINDA ADDISON: THE QUEEN OF HORROR PROSE & POETRY

ELLEN DATLOW: HORROR ANTHOLOGIST/EDITOR QUEEN

Paul Tremblay

I'll never forget how I discovered Paul Tremblay's work. Stephen King tweeted, "A HEAD FULL OF GHOSTS, by Paul Tremblay: Scared the living hell out of me, and I'm pretty hard to scare."

Of course, I had to have it. I put it on a list of "to buy" books, and the next time I found myself in a bookstore, I bought it. Read it almost immediately, and it promptly scared the shit out of me, just like Stephen King warned his Constant Readers it would. It's demon possession horror, which is the number one scariest subgenre for me (followed by cult [folk] horror at number two).

From there, I decided that Tremblay is a new favorite horror author, and I read everything he releases, like *Disappearance at Devil's Rock*. It's a haunting missing person, coming-of-age story that breaks my heart in two. I felt actual anger toward Paul Tremblay for hurting me with this book.

His latest release, *The Pallbearers Club*, is Tremblay at his most Tremblayish. It's a faux memoir that feels autobiographical, about Art Barbara, who claims in the first sentence, "I am not Art Barbara." Art Barbara, who is not Art Barbara, gives an account of a season of his life; the pages contradict his narrative. The margins are littered with notes from someone we come to know as Mercy—an older, confident, more worldly young woman who befriends Art. These notes and corrections serve to undermine the reader's faith in Art's tale. Tremblay ultimately crafts a relationship between himself, these two characters, and the reader in a way that I have never experienced before.

Tremblay has a unique take on horror—the fear of ourselves: who we are, what we're capable of, and how we haunt our own minds and the lives of those around us.

Photo by Cheryl Murphy

RECOMMENDED TITLES

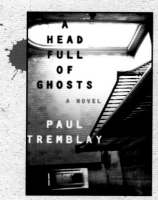

A HEAD FULL OF GHOSTS (2015)
demon possession; family dramas; reality TV

THE PALLBEARERS CLUB (2022)
meta-fiction; coming-of-age; identity crisis

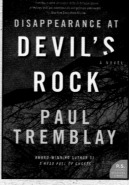

DISAPPEARANCE AT DEVIL'S ROCK (2016)
missing person; coming-of-age; mystery

GROWING THINGS (2019)
short story collection

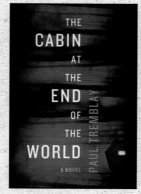

THE CABIN AT THE END OF THE WORLD (2018)
home invasion; family; apocalyptic

SURVIVOR SONG (2020)
global pandemic; apocalyptic; "zombies"

Paul Tremblay Recommends: "How could I possibly pick only three? Torture! But wonderful torture. Shirley Jackson's *The Haunting of Hill House* because we're all haunted. Clive Barker's *Books of Blood, Volume 1* because he dares go there. Mark Danielewski's *House of Leaves* because its horror is still expanding."

Cults

You're in a cult. Call your dad.

—Karen Kilgariff, My Favorite Murder Podcast

I have a strong affinity for books centered on alternative religions and cults, with a caveat: It needs to be believable. If readers are being asked to invest in characters that will ultimately exhibit strange behaviors or take part in life-threatening rituals, I need to know why. How did these people get here? Why do they believe in something so outside the norm to the point of devoting their whole way of life to it? In my opinion, for books in this subgenre to stick the landing, the author has the responsibility of convincing the reader that the cult leader is charismatic, persuasive, and manipulative enough to get seemingly rational people to abandon traditional forms of religion and worship far more alternative practices.

I love when authors rip down the veil to reveal what goes on behind closed doors. All the dark liturgy, ritualistic sacrifices, and underground, secret meetings are exposed to the reader. It's fascinating. We all have a morbid curiosity about things that seem taboo or scandalous. It's where the term "rubbernecking" comes from and why we sit in bumper-to-bumper traffic after an accident. Everyone has to slow down and take a hard look at the chaos. It is the same when we are exposed to the secret things that happen behind the closed doors of a cult.

We cannot look away. We must satisfy all the speculation and the burning questions. Just how far did these people go? It almost always boils down to the same hard truths. Inside each of us is that intrinsic sense of belonging to something bigger than us. We wish, deep down, to be part of a community of like-minded people and possibly even a greater power than ourselves. Cult leaders understand this about human nature, and they prey on it. This dynamic makes for some compelling horror stories.

It was hard to narrow my selections down to just include a few, so these books are my favorites.

BENEATH

BY KRISTI DEMEESTER (2017)

Jesus had not saved Cora before. He would not save her now. There were only her own two hands and the blade tucked into her palm. If there was a savior for her, it was made up of hard, glinting metal.

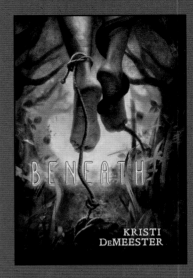

KRISTI
DeMEESTER

This was the first small press book I requested for review. I saw the book cover and the synopsis in a listicle (article + book list), and it sounded like something I would like to read and review for my growing "Bookstagram" platform. So, I mustered up the courage to email the publisher, Word Horde, for a review copy, and they graciously sent me this book and several others. Bless small presses.

Cora Mayburn, a journalist, is told she is going to rural Appalachia on assignment to investigate a story about a snake-handling cult. Fundamentalist, religious abuse is something she had to wrestle with in her past, so this particular assignment weighs heavily on her.

She meets a young "preacher man" named Michael, and they become fast friends. Readers will become immediately invested in their growing relationship.

Dark and disturbing, the prose is absorbing. DeMeester uses different perspectives to create layers of mystery and secrets. Cora maintains her professional, journalistic approach at first, but then that veneer begins to dissolve as she becomes sucked into the affairs of the strange townsfolk.

The storyline blends a variety of horror subgenres, which makes *Beneath* a book with mass appeal. There's psychological horror, the depravity of religion gone off the rails, monsters, creatures, snakes (I know there are readers out there who are petrified of snakes), and, lastly, good old-fashioned body horror.

Kristi DeMeester's signature contribution to horror is empowering her female protagonists with plenty of charisma, strength, and capability to face their demons while also fighting evil. *Beneath* is no exception.

AT A GLANCE

THEMES: Snake handlers, journalism, investigations, religious trauma, sexual abuse, motherhood

TONE: Bleak, Dark, Disturbing, Intensifying Dread, Suspenseful

STYLE: Multiple POV

SETTING: Rural Appalachia

PUBLISHER: Indie/Word Horde

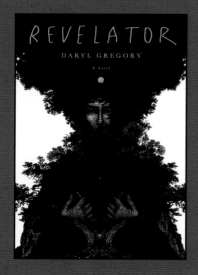

REVELATOR

BY DARYL GREGORY (2021)

They acted like they were meeting royalty, and in a way they were. They were the elders of the Church of the God in the Mountain, her uncles and cousins, all Birches by blood — and she was their Revelator.

AT A GLANCE

THEMES: Bootleggers, family dynamics, secrets, gods, religion, the Bible, male dominance, racism, religious oppression, "chosen one," identity

TONE: Disturbing, Eerie, Intensifying Dread

STYLE: Character-Driven, Cinematic, Dual Timeline, Intricately Plotted

SETTING: Tennessee (1930–1948)

PUBLISHER: Traditional/ Knopf Publishing Group

Aside from being an iconic horror book, *Revelator* is one of the best books I've ever read, period. An intricately crafted, richly detailed story about a young woman named Stella Birch Wallace, who is running a successful bootlegging outfit in 1948 when she gets word of her grandmother's passing. She must return to the family farm where she grew up to check on a young girl named Sunny before the rest of her family gets there. I fell in love with tough-as-nails Stella Birch Wallace and I know you will too.

A dual timeline from 1933 follows Stella's upbringing at the farm. Her father leaves Stella in his mother's care—a stoic woman named Motty Birch—while he goes to look for work. Stella is required to help Motty tend to the farm, as well as fulfill religious duties for her family. They worship the God in the Mountain, intimately and secretively known as Ghostdaddy. Motty and Stella are Revelators: an integral role as the lifeblood of their family's religion.

As the intensifying tale unfolds between the two timelines, the saga of this family's secret, insular faith, and worship of this deity in the mountain builds to a mind-blowing crescendo. The entire time I was reading this book, I was in awe of Daryl Gregory's talent. This book shot its way to the top of my very treasured and most selective "Top 10 Books of All Time" honor.

THE TWISTED ONES

BY T. KINGFISHER (2019)

Don't start crazymaking. You're alone in a house in the middle of nowhere with a bunch of dolls. If there was ever a time to not start down the horror-movie road, this is it.

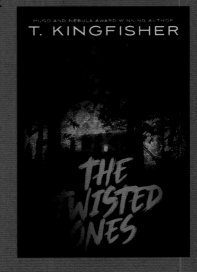

Imagine sleeping over at your dead grandmother's house in the middle of nowhere. She was a horrible, mean person, so there are no warm, fuzzy feelings being in the house. There's an entire room filled with her doll collection, and her ex-husband, not your grandpa, left a creepy journal on the bedside table that you read at night because there is no other source of entertainment. Your cell phone doesn't have a signal. There's no Wi-Fi or cable TV.

Oh, and your dog wakes you up in the middle of the night to bark at something outside. Every night.

This is the premise of *The Twisted Ones* by T. Kingfisher.

Mouse and Bongo. I will never forget these two. Mouse is the nickname given to the young woman narrating this story in a first-person point of view, and Bongo is her dog.

Mouse's father is physically unable to take care of his mother's estate when she passes away, so Mouse must make the trip out to rural North Carolina to get affairs in order. When she opens the door and finds crap stacked from floor to ceiling, she understands she's going to have to stay longer than she anticipated. When she's not hauling the trash from the house out to the dumps, Mouse and Bongo explore the woods surrounding her grandmother's house. With every passing day, things get weirder and weirder until you're almost screaming at the book's pages for Mouse to get Bongo in the truck and get the fuck out of there. The way things build up slowly over time is pure horror bliss.

AT A GLANCE

THEMES: Hoarders, creepy woods, isolation, dementia, family relationships, strange sightings, things that go "bump" in the night, dolls, man's best friend, strange phenomena

TONE: Dark, Disorienting, Eerie, Humorous, Intensifying Dread, Menacing

STYLE: Character-Driven, First-Person POV, Leisurely Paced

SETTING: North Carolina

PUBLISHER: Traditional/Saga Press

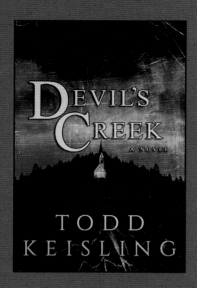

DEVIL'S CREEK

BY TODD KEISLING (2020)

With Skynyrd blaring through the speakers and a full tank of gas, life couldn't get any better. And it wouldn't. Waylon would be dead before the sun rose again.

Todd Keisling's *Devil's Creek* is the perfect example of quality cult horror. Keisling lays down important, historical groundwork for the setting of his epic cult tale.

Stauford, Kentucky is a fictional small town haunted by the legend of Jacob Masters' death cult, The Lord's Church of Holy Voices, in which the townspeople worshipped a nameless deity in a church at Devil's Creek. The history of this congregation ends in tragedy. A fire kills everyone except "The Stauford Six."

Thirty years later, The Six have grown up and moved on. One of The Six, Jack Tremly, must return to his small hometown to take care of his grandmother's estate and is revisited by the history of Devil's Creek.

Keisling spends quality time peeling back the layers of this seemingly quaint town to reveal the dark, insidious roots below. Told in five parts, readers can expect to witness graphically detailed accounts of cult practices led by a murderous, sexual deviant. Some of it is pretty difficult to stomach. At no point in this novel did I feel as though I was enduring the depravity needlessly. Keisling's story development is given top priority. Suffering through explicit scenes felt necessary instead of exploitive or gratuitous, and every character was given a reason to exist on the page. This is quintessential cult horror inspired by horror legends King and Lovecraft. Cosmic, cult, character-driven horror at its finest.

AT A GLANCE

THEMES: Homecoming, sacrifices, families, children, murder, summoning a god, the woods

TONE: Atmospheric, Bleak, Blood-Soaked, Brutal, Dark, Disturbing, Eerie, Gruesome, Intensifying Dread, Menacing, Shocking, Suspenseful, Violent

STYLE: Brisk Pacing, Character-Driven, Cinematic, Intricately Plotted, Multiple POV, Stephen King(ish)

SETTING: Kentucky

PUBLISHER: Indie/Silver Shamrock Publishing; Cemetery Dance Publications (2023)

MEXICAN GOTHIC

BY SILVIA MORENO-GARCIA (2020)

The walls speak to me. They tell me secrets. Don't listen to them, press your hands against your ears, Noemí. There are ghosts. They're real. You'll see them eventually.

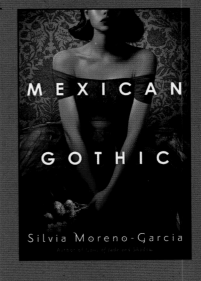

This book is full of surprises. In classic Gothic horror fashion, this book is what readers generally refer to as a "slow burn," but I'm going to take it a step further and add a caveat: It's a slow burn, yes, but there's enough drama and mystery to keep it moving. Slow burns usually demand readers adjust their urgency to stay in step with a slowed-down pace, but it's my opinion that Silvia Moreno-Garcia wrote this Gothic storyline at a lively pace. I was never found wanting; there was never a dull moment or lag.

Noemí Taboada is a young, beautiful socialite in the 1950s. One night, she comes home after a party to a troubling letter from her cousin, who recently married into a mysterious family living in the Mexican countryside.

Noemí is to make a trip to the estate to check in on her cousin.

As soon as Noemí arrives at High Place, she wastes no time asserting herself in the lives of the residents there. She makes it very clear that her purpose is to serve her cousin, who reached out to her in distress—she's not interested in the family's demands for secrecy or adherence to their strange rules and traditions. At night, Noemí suffers from delusions and nightmares. She sees strange symbols, and sometimes the wallpaper seems to alter its pattern right before her eyes. A trick of the light or did someone slip something in her drink?

The residents at High Place are an unseemly lot, and everyone seems like they're hiding something.

I fell in love with Noemí. At first, she seemed a little spoiled and too self-absorbed to take on this rescue mission, but over time, Noemí's confidence and "take-no-shit" attitude scored major points with me. I also enjoyed the romance at this Gothic tale's core. Horror with romance is always a plus, and I long for more of it.

AT A GLANCE

THEMES: Family, estates, secrets, lies, sickness, cousins, newlyweds, nightmares, hallucinations, fungi, Mexico, socialites, young women, rural living, patriarchal families, traditions, sacrifice

TONE: Atmospheric, Disorienting, Eerie, Humorous, Intensifying Dread, Menacing

STYLE: Character-Driven, Cinematic, Intricately Plotted, Leisurely Paced

SETTING: Mexico (the 1950s)

PUBLISHER: Traditional/Del Rey Books

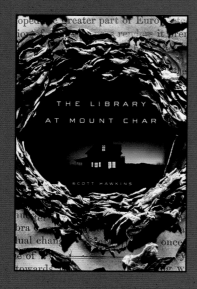

THE LIBRARY AT MOUNT CHAR

BY SCOTT HAWKINS (2015)

Her fingertips trembled with the memory of faint, fading vibrations carried down the shaft of a brass spear, and in her heart, the hate of them blazed like a black sun.

AT A GLANCE

THEMES: Gods and goddesses, kidnapped, imprisonment, torture, magic, secrets, legacy, creation, unique gifts and powers, libraries

TONE: Brutal, Disorienting, Gruesome, Humorous, Intensifying Dread, Shocking, Violent

STYLE: Brisk Pacing, Character-Driven, First-Person POV, Intricately Plotted, Multiple POV

SETTING: America/Garrison Oaks

PUBLISHER: Traditional/Crown

This book defies genre labeling. It's an odd book. My reading experience was similar to the way I felt while I was enjoying *The Phantom Tollbooth* or *A Wrinkle in Time*—equal parts fascination/wonder and confusion. I marveled at the imagination of author Scott Hawkins. The comparisons to Neil Gaiman are spot on. Is it a fantasy book? Science fiction? Who cares. Today, it's horror, and all you need to know is that you need to read it before you're murdered.

There are so many moving parts and important aspects of this story that it's difficult to know where to begin explaining what it's about. Since I'm including it in a list of horror books, I suppose I should start with the villain, Adam Black, or "Father" as his "students/children" call him. Father kidnapped people and brought them back to his Library to train them to become gods. He forced these gods-in-training to adapt to his ancient customs, punishing them with instruments of torture when they failed to live up to his expectations.

Now he's missing, possibly dead, and the gods must solve the mystery of his disappearance, suffer through their intense sibling rivalries, and determine what will happen to the Library and Father's legacy.

The mythology and world-building are extreme at first. You'll be tempted to feel like you're not up for the challenge, but press on! The reward is in the emotional ride you're on while reading this book.

The best horror is provocative—something that shocks readers into absorbing the story into the hindbrain so that thinking about it becomes as normal as all of your daily functions. Hawkins provides his audience with the opportunity to ponder life as shades of gray instead of black and white. No good or evil . . . just good people who do bad things, or bad people who are capable of good.

LITTLE EVE

BY CATRIONA WARD (2018)

"So many questions asked about what I did that night," I say. "No one has asked, what did that night do to me?"

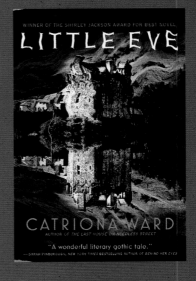

I wanted to live in the pages of this book and never, ever leave. My reading experience was so vivid and delicious, I can recall the way it made me feel just by thinking of the book. Even now, as I type this, the imagery, the mood, they're rushing back to me, flooding my mind with scenes of a turbulent sea, an isolated crumbling castle called Altnaharra, and the soggy, bleak landscape of Scotland.

I feel a sense of longing, almost as if I miss the story. I don't often re-read my books because there are too many new books to enjoy, but I know I will return to *Little Eve*.

This is a story told in reverse, beginning with the ritualistic murder of a strange, isolated family; their bodies are discovered by someone who lives in the neighboring town. He finds one survivor, a woman named Dinah. Dinah eventually tells her tale in court, implicating one person: Little Eve. The case is especially intriguing to Chief Inspector Black, who decides to investigate, giving special attention to the family's leader, the one they call The Adder, or "Uncle."

Little Eve is peak gothic vibes. It won the Shirley Jackson Award in 2018 (the year it was originally released in the UK). It wins everything for me. I give it all the awards in my heart. My biggest praise goes to Catriona Ward for detailing the cult and its practices for her readers. As I've mentioned, if I am to understand why cult members behave the way they do, it's essential to witness the psychological manipulation and intricate religious practices of the cult in order to make sense of it all. And Ward delivers in spades.

Readers who love a complicated murder mystery, strange religious cults, and strong female protagonists will likely fall in love with *Little Eve* as hard as I did.

AT A GLANCE

THEMES: Children raised in a doomsday snake cult/commune, ritualistic religious practices, isolation, patriarchal oppression, pregnancy, forced sex, murder mystery

TONE: Atmospheric, Eerie, Intensifying Dread, Shocking, Suspenseful

STYLE: Character-driven, Critically Acclaimed, Dual Timeline, Intricately Plotted, Lyrical, Multiple POV

SETTING: Scotland

PUBLISHER: Traditional/ Weidenfeld & Nicolson (U.K. edition); Tor Nightfire (U.S. edition, 2022)

Adam Nevill

Adam Nevill writes the scariest modern horror books. Period. This man has his finger on something inherently evil, and it shows up in all his work: insidious, bone-chilling, hair-raising, spine-tingling terror. Every single one of his books that I have read has scared me to the point of actually being scared. Does that make sense? When I'm reading a book and it's starting to freak me out, I can put a bookmark in it and walk away. I can empty the dishwasher or take the dog for a walk and quickly get over those creepy feelings. Adam Nevill's books don't allow for this. I have tried, but something prevented me. A dark, sinister presence made me keep reading, and then I was too scared to sleep. He has given me nightmares.

I'm not saying that Nevill is some kind of horror-writing warlock who curses his readership, but I'm not NOT saying it either.

I mean, have you read *The Ritual*? That was the first book of Nevill's I read. It's about these friends with all of this unsettled tension between them going on a backpacking trip deep into the Scandinavian wilderness. The men are distracted by their emotions, pain, and anger, so they are missing clues that something is very wrong with the woods. But the reader sees the clues, and there's nothing you can do to stop the horror. It's exhilarating, awful, and terrifying.

Last Days might be his scariest. These indie documentarians are filming footage during their investigation into an old ritualistic cult massacre. They have no idea about the evil they are uncovering. Actually, wait, no. *Cunning Folk* is the scariest because there's a jump scare in it. You know how in movies something happens that makes your skin crawl with fear, something that startles you and makes your heart race? Nevill manages to induce a jump scare in a book. Never experienced one? Read *Cunning Folk*. Oh, and there's also a scene in *The Reddening* that made me gasp, and then my stupid brain kept reading the horrific passage repeatedly. I just couldn't get over it. My mind was reeling with horror.

Trust me, when I say he writes the scariest modern horror books today . . . he does. I show up to his books to be scared.

RECOMMENDED TITLES

THE RITUAL (2011)
scary woods; cults; folk horror

LAST DAYS (2012)
documentary investigation; cults

THE REDDENING (2019)
strong women; cults; folk horror

CUNNING FOLK (2021)
new house in the woods; cults, folk horror, scary neighbors

APARTMENT 16 (2010)
haunted house; mystery

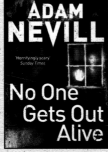

NO ONE GETS OUT ALIVE (2014)
haunted house

HOUSE OF SMALL SHADOWS (2013)
creepy dolls; puppets; taxidermy; haunted house

WYRD AND OTHER DERELICTIONS (2020)
experimental; no characters—only setting/place

Adam Nevill Recommends: "*Ghost Stories of an Antiquary*, by M R James, set fire to my imagination when I was a child and, whenever I was alone, introduced the possibility of uncanny presences into my daily existence. The stories were read to me. His influence is in the DNA of everything I've since conceived. *War of the Worlds* by H. G. Wells triggered my innate feelings of cosmic terror soon afterward. By the time I'd read H. P. Lovecraft's *Dagon and Other Macabre Tales*, I was certain that doing anything other than trying to achieve the same effects in my own stories would leave me dissatisfied. This early exposure to critically acclaimed horror charted the course of my life."

Slashers & Serial Killers

When people tell me that they have yet to read a horror book that actually scared them, I oftentimes lead them here. Graphic violence is scary. I know that might not always be the case with slasher movies—a lot of them are black comedies or satirical, using humor as a counterweight to balance out the terror. Don't expect that here.

The following books are probably the most disturbing books on the list. As they should be; they're the closest to the real-life horrors in daily headlines and true crime podcasts. Horror fiction reflects back to us our fears and trauma. When we read stories about a maniacal killer on a violent rampage hunting down their next victims, we engage with our most primal instincts in a safe environment.

We're able to feel empathy for the characters who find themselves in a frightening, life-threatening situation. We hope for their survival. In fact, I'm a strong believer that empathy is one of the main feelings on tap during almost any horror reading experience. Investing in the lives of fictional characters as they go through trauma exercises those heart muscles. That desperation to see another human being (even though they are fictional) find their way out of hopelessness is a good thing.

But a few of these books also explore the origin stories of their characters who kill. And this is where the really disturbing elements come in. We are inside the minds of killers. We are given insight into the psychology of a predator, and it's a scary, unsettling place to be. It's easy to empathize with all the victims in the story, but troubling when we find ourselves empathizing with or relating to the psycho-killer. That's horror.

These books are "all the trigger warnings" rolled into one; nothing funny or lighthearted found here. The violence is not used for "shock and awe" value. It's not cartoonish, or cute, or comic-book style. So, buckle-up.

I'm giving you recommendations for pure, unadulterated horror. Enjoy.

GRIND YOUR BONES TO DUST

BY NICHOLAS DAY (2019)

Louis ran through the dark because he did not want to die screaming while being torn apart and eaten alive.

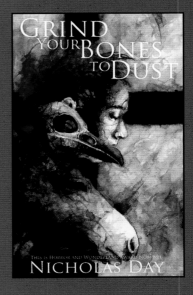

I don't know if Nicholas Day sold his soul at a crossroads to give us *Grind Your Bones to Dust*, but this book feels like the result of a pact made with the Devil. Some parts are so horrifying that I almost wish I could spare you from this recommendation, but horror demands engagement with darkness, and this one is pitch black.

I can say with confidence that James Hayte is a villain so unfathomably evil that he is the single most wicked character to ever terrify me in literature (second only to Cormac McCarthy's the Judge in *Blood Meridian*). There are murderous deeds committed against innocent people that will make you very uncomfortable. Nicholas Day writes them in such a way that you are unlikely to ever forget a single one. Part of me wishes I could scrub them from my mind, and part of me wants to applaud Day for being the kind of author who knows how to write exceptionally memorable acts of violence. He understands that sometimes full detail is not required to project a horrifying act into a reader's mind. Things can be suggested with just the right words, and it's more unsettling than full disclosure could ever be.

At some point, James is joined by Billings, a supernatural raven who speaks in these prophetic parables and mysteries. The scenes with Billings and James are some of my favorite storytelling moments.

The best part of this book is that it's thought-provoking. You will ponder the nature of God, the purpose of religion, the depravity of man, and the hopelessness of a life without love. Maybe you'll even experience a bit of an existential crisis.

This is true horror at its core. It's unapologetically graphic and insensitive. It will offend and disgust. While it is an unforgettable journey through a bleak landscape full of terrors, at the end of it all, you'll shelve this book among your favorites.

AT A GLANCE

THEMES: Pain, suffering, death, serial killer, friendship, hell on earth, religious trauma, love, hate, murder, murderous animals

TONE: Bleak, Blood-Soaked, Dark, Gruesome, Melancholy, Menacing, Violent

STYLE: Brisk Pacing, Critically Acclaimed, Intricately Plotted, Lyrical

SETTING: Oregon

PUBLISHER: Indie/Excession Press; Rooster Republic

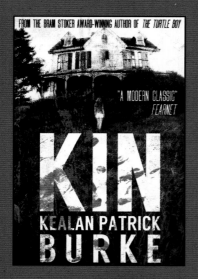

KIN

BY KEALAN PATRICK BURKE (2011)

*If you're hell-bent on lookin' for fairness,
you're on the wrong damn planet.*

This book is the closest I have come to watching a scary movie. I don't watch scary movies, so this is the next best thing.

Burke has an astonishing skill of bringing the reader into the story with technicolor descriptive language. There were times in the beginning I was unsure if I wanted to keep going.

Claire Lambert is the sole survivor of a massacre that claimed the lives of her friends. As she begins to heal from this brutal tragedy, her desire for revenge becomes more than just a fantasy. Against all logic, Claire makes a journey back to Elkwood, where her brutal suffering took place, on a mission to right the injustices of the horrors that haunt her and avenge the senseless murders of the ones she lost.

This story has way more to do with the aftermath of a sadistic tragedy rather than the tragedy itself. Sure, there is the suspense, the cringe-worthy disgusting moments, the nasty characters, the gore, and the danger, but the main themes for me went way deeper than the entertainment—I was moved to tears a few times.

This is the novel that minted Burke as a favorite author of mine.

AT A GLANCE

 GRL PWR

THEMES: Survivor's guilt, brutal murder, cannibalism, PTSD, soldiers, domestic abuse, revenge, vengeance, vigilante justice, grief, rage, trauma, a family of killers, rural living

TONE: Blood-Soaked, Brutal, Dark, Disturbing, Gruesome, Suspenseful

STYLE: Brisk Pacing, Character-Driven, Cinematic

SETTING: Alabama

PUBLISHER: Indie/Self-Published

TRUE CRIME

BY SAMANTHA KOLESNIK (2020)

There was no evil in the world that was not man's work.

Samantha Kolesnik's debut hurts like unrelenting thumb pressure on a fresh bruise; an unflinching, brave story about identity. A fictional account of siblings raised by human monsters and enduring physical, emotional, and sexual abuse of the most violent kind. Readers will have to bear witness to some horrific accounts, but almost more troubling are the lasting effects and consequences trauma has on the human psyche, especially in the formative years. This is a novella, so thankfully, the story doesn't focus on actual scenes of parent/child abuse for too long. It's extreme horror, is what I'm telling you. I debated putting it on this list, but you know, my reader's heart wouldn't let me leave it off. It's worthy of praise. It's unabashedly horror and quite frankly, brilliant.

Once Lim and Suzy venture out on their own, the author does a masterful job of portraying the different ways victimhood manifests itself. Suzy is our first-person narrator, so the reader gets an intimate look inside the chaos of her damaged mind. Suzy's brother, Lim, displays all the external signs of his internal turmoil, but it's really Suzy that the author hones in on, and it's some of the most powerful storytelling I have ever read.

Samantha Kolesnik writes scenes of dazzling beauty that stand out like a beacon of light in pitch black. Most memorable for me were the "Creators" and the "Builders" that come along with Suzy in an attempt to help her on her journey toward recovery. These scenes were like little treasures that made all the ugliness in this story worth the pain of enduring. I can't and I won't tell you what happens to Suzy in the end. You really must read this one for yourself. I promise it's worth the struggle. What a remarkable debut novel.

AT A GLANCE

THEMES: Sexual abuse, psychological abuse, child abuse, vengence, killers, identity, brothers and sisters, mothers and daughters, cutting, murder, torture, animal cruelty, sex workers, death, social commentary

TONE: Bleak, Blood-Soaked, Brutal, Gruesome, Shocking, Violent

STYLE: Brisk Pacing, Character-Driven, Cinematic, Intricately Plotted

SETTING: "The South"

PUBLISHER: Indie/Grindhouse Press

CAMP SLAUGHTER

BY SERGIO GOMEZ (2019)

We should have just fucking gone to Puerto Rico instead.

Camp Slaughter is the self-published debut book from Sergio Gomez that convinced me the slasher genre can rise above the stereotypes. In my experience, most slasher books have a large cast of underdeveloped characters for the "psycho killer" to have plenty of people to hunt, maim, and kill. I've also found that slasher fiction isn't too concerned with the plot, leaning heavily on violence as the primary vehicle for entertaining readers. Not my favorite brand of horror, but it does have its audience.

However, Sergio Gomez wastes zero time getting his readers invested in his characters. I noticed this right away. He spends time with them, brings them to life for us, and makes us care. Which is dangerous. It's so dangerous to care about the characters in a slasher novel, right?

Here's the real curveball: You'll care about the psycho killer too. His name is Ignacio.

Through some impressive storytelling, told in flashbacks, we get to see Ignacio's past. Gomez infuses these scenes with detailed imagery and a rich, cultural backdrop, making Ignacio a sympathetic antagonist. He's a killer with a name and a backstory who is going to unleash some fresh hell on these teens who show up at a cabin for a weekend getaway. What could be more entertaining than that?

AT A GLANCE

THEMES: Cabin in the woods, weekend getaway, vacation, college-aged adults, cannibalism

TONE: Bleak, Blood-Soaked, Brutal, Intensifying Dread, Menacing, Violent

STYLE: Brisk Pacing, Character-Driven, Multiple POV

SETTING: Pennsylvania

PUBLISHER: Indie/Self-Published

GOTH

BY OTSUICHI (2002)

Morino and I had a unique way of life that was well beyond the ordinary. Exchanging pictures of corpses was simply part of this.

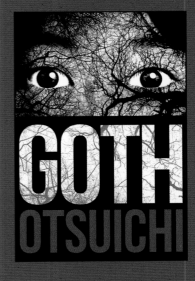

The narrator (unnamed) and his friend Yoru Morino form a friendship centered on their fascination with the macabre, death, and killers. They are both socially awkward people, keeping to themselves or each other at school. After school hours, they investigate murders and visit crime scenes.

Goth is formatted a bit like the book *Penpal* (page 70) with connected vignettes that tell a whole story. The subject matter is deeply disturbing but written in such a way that makes it impossible to stop reading. Once you read the first story, plan on doing nothing else with your life until you turn the last page. Every story is pitch-perfect, detailing an account of a killer and our protagonist's involvement with them. The last story, "Voice," is unlike anything I've ever read before, setting the vibrancy and beauty of life as a stark contrast to the darkness of someone brutally stealing that life.

There is a fair amount of animal cruelty in some of these stories. It's easy to just skim over it and find a place to resume without losing any sense of what's happening in the story. In the afterward(s), which you must read because they're endearing and hilarious, the author mentions how he wants people to know that the killers in the story are monsters, "youkai" (a supernatural entity). They're not human. The male protagonist/narrator is a youkai too, with the same powers as the killers. The female protagonist, Morino, has psychic abilities, which is why she attracted the youkai to her and why they are friends. Everything is set in a fictional world, not our world. It was important for Otsuichi to explain this to readers, so I'm setting up early expectations for you going into this masterclass in pitch-black horror, depravity, and suspense.

AT A GLANCE

THEMES: Animal cruelty, death, morbid fascinations, serial killers, antisocial personalities, suicide, the mind of a killer, child death, murder, detailed crime scenes, grief, trauma, siblings, childhood, school, teens, investigations, journal

TONE: Bleak, Blood-Soaked, Brutal, Disturbing, Eerie, Intensifying Dread, Violent

STYLE: Cinematic, First-Person POV, Intricately Plotted, Multiple POV, Vignettes

SETTING: Japan

PUBLISHER: Traditional/ Kadokawa Shoten (Japanese); Haikasoru (English translation, 2015)

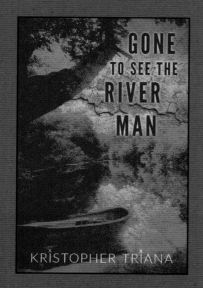

GONE TO SEE THE RIVER MAN

BY KRISTOPHER TRIANA (2020)

The people we make suffer stay inside of us longer and more deeply than those who we bring joy, don't you think?

AT A GLANCE

THEMES: Prison inmates, serial killers, prison pen pals, racially targeted killings, incest, mental disabilities, demons, cruelty, perverted love, psychologically damaged people, infatuation, obsession, loyalty, sadism

TONE: Bleak, Blood-Soaked, Brutal, Disturbing, Shocking, Violent

STYLE: Brisk Pacing, Character-Driven, Cinematic, Intricately Plotted

SETTING: N/A

PUBLISHER: Indie/Grindhouse Press

This is likely the darkest, most extreme book on the list. **Proceed with caution**. I'm tempted to just let the list of trigger warnings roll out like a scroll so potential readers can make an informed decision, but I will be as detailed as I can be in the "At a Glance" section so you know what you're getting into with this one. I do like it very gruesome sometimes. A few of my favorite books by some of my favorite authors won't make this list because they're not acceptable for mixed company. Maybe I'll write a book down the road for extreme horror recommendations?

This is the story of a woman named Lori who has an unhealthy infatuation with a prison inmate named Edmund. He's not your garden variety "one and done" murderer. Edmund did unspeakable things to his female victims. It's inconceivable why our protagonist Lori is so enamored with him.

As the story progresses and the intimacy between Lori and Edmund grows, he eventually asks her to go on an errand and she accepts. She sees his request as a test of her love and loyalty. She brings along her older sister, Abby, who suffers mentally and physically from a childhood accident. The reader learns more and more about Lori as she embarks on her mysterious errand to prove to her new flame that she's serious about her love for him.

A fiercely compelling, addictive storyline that marches right up to the conclusion and bares down on any hope of redemption the reader has left. I was left feeling both gutted and satisfied.

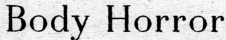

Body Horror

The definition of "body horror" is pretty succinct: violations of the human body. I mean, that's pretty much it. I would just point to author Clive Barker and director David Cronenberg and tell you that those two legends are the blueprints for body horror. They have laid the foundation and built the framework from which all body horror fiction to follow will draw inspiration. Sure, Cronenberg is a movie director, but visuals from his movies are influential on horror fiction and how writers describe scenes of grotesque bodily transformations.

But even Cronenberg and Barker have body horror inspirations, I'm sure, and people who know the genre better than I do likely have their opinions on the true origins. I mean, Mary Shelley's *Frankenstein* is literally a story about a monster cobbled together with body parts from multiple corpses, right? That's body horror.

Think about your own body for a moment. How well do you really know it? All of our basic, bodily functions are automatic; our bodies run on systems of organs, oxygen, and circulation all on their own with no real help from our consciousness. Viruses, diseases, and toxins come in and out without our knowledge. Our bodies fight these daily battles while we're busy grocery shopping or reading a book. Body horror imagines what would happen if there were people in the world consumed with body modification to serve evil purposes: cults obsessed with mutilating their own bodies, deranged scientists that delight in experimenting on human bodies, medical labs and test tubes, parasites and intestinal worms. Are you squirming?

Read these books and you'll never trust your body is safe ever again.

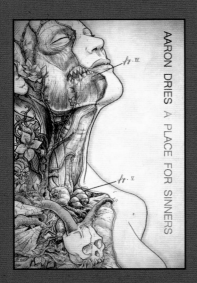

A PLACE FOR SINNERS

BY AARON DRIES (2014)

The sky was purple and freckled with the evening's first stars. Robert had read somewhere that it took hundreds—or was it thousands?—of years for light to reach human eyes on Earth. How disappointing for the star to have traveled millions of miles through space and time, only to illuminate places where grace had never touched. Some of those stars would be dead by now. He was warmed by their ghosts.

I'm taking you far off the beaten path for this one, a book I'm quite sure you've never heard of before. *A Place for Sinners* is one thousand different ways to be scared. The author's wheelhouse is submerging the reader into the atmosphere of the story—in this case, a suffocating jungle setting—while simultaneously preying on your worst psychological fears. Needless to say, I was anxious and emotionally unhinged the entire time I read this book.

Amity and her brother Caleb live with their mother in Australia. Caleb is overly protective of his sister because of a childhood tragedy that scarred the family and caused Amity's total loss of hearing. The siblings decide to adventure together to the jungles of Thailand. They end up on a boat tour to a remote island and are looking forward to exploring nature. However, the tour group doesn't know what is waiting for them there: violence and misery.

Amity and Caleb face the antagonist of this story, Susan Sycamore, who is worse than any kind of natural disaster. I will never forget this character. Dries tells the story of *A Place for Sinners* with multiple points of view, one of which is from Susan's voice. Being with her, in her mind, is a terrifying, awful place to be. The ways in which she has modified her body to become an apex predator is terrifying and gross. You can't help but visualize what she has done to herself in your mind, and you won't stop thinking about it even after you've finished reading.

This book is an unflinching, unsettling kind of horror. The reader looks straight into the face of madness and cannot look away. An utterly brutal story of survival and loss, *A Place for Sinners* proves Aaron Dries to be an underrated force in horror storytelling.

AT A GLANCE

THEMES: Traveling, vacations, missing person, family, siblings, psychopaths, jungles, killers, isolation, adventure, tourists

TONE: Bleak, Blood-Soaked, Brutal, Disturbing, Intensifying Dread, Shocking, Violent

STYLE: Brisk Pacing, Character-Driven, Cinematic, Intricately Plotted, Lyrical, Multiple POV

SETTING: Australia/Thailand

PUBLISHER: Indie/Samhain Publishing; Self-Published (2020)

TRANSMUTED

BY EVE HARMS (2021)

I can't control it. I can't control what they'll see and how they'll think about me. What's the point of hiding?

I mention in another book recommendation how women are over-qualified to write horror. Our very existence is threatened every damn day. I worry about us. I worry about trans women and how some people's whole purpose in life is to erase them. It terrifies me right now to even type a statement like that, but it's true. Why can't trans women just live their lives in peace and happiness?

Transmuted begins with the reader joining Isa in her personal struggles as a trans woman waiting to undergo facial feminization surgery. She has a complicated relationship with her family that becomes even more strained when Isa is asked to forfeit her medical procedure savings to save her estranged father's life.

Desperate to look and feel more feminine, Isa resorts to some radical, experimental testing in order to complete her transition. It's difficult to watch Isa make hasty, risky decisions, but it's also understandable. Harms does an excellent job of communicating the social pressures and emotional anxiety that force Isa into the dangerous circumstances she finds herself in.

Eventually, *Transmuted* rockets into full-blown body-horror reminiscent of *The Island of Dr. Moreau.*

Eve Harms has a warm, welcoming, and accessible storytelling voice that effortlessly penetrates past the page to grab hold of her audience and tell a story that will live in readers' hearts for a long, long time.

AT A GLANCE

 GRL PWR

THEMES: Transphobia, deadnames, fat-shaming, violence, torture, experimental medical procedures, death and dying, family dysfunction

TONE: Dark, Disturbing, Gruesome, Intensifying Dread, Menacing, Shocking, Suspenseful

STYLE: Brisk Pacing, Character-Driven, Cinematic

SETTING: Los Angeles

PUBLISHER: Indie/Unnerving Books

LAST DAYS

BY BRIAN EVENSON (2009)

How much weirder, thought Kline, is it possible for my life to get? And then he pushed the thought down and tried to ignore it, afraid of what the answer might be.

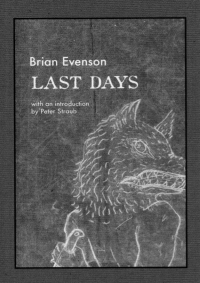

AT A GLANCE

THEMES: Murder, investigation, self-mutilation, kidnapping, detective work, crime scenes, brotherhood, amputations, human nature, identity

TONE: Disturbing, Humorous, Intensifying Dread, Menacing, Suspenseful, Violent

STYLE: Brisk Pacing, Character-Driven, Cinematic, Critically Acclaimed, Intricately Plotted

SETTING: N/A

PUBLISHER: Indie/Underland Press; Coffee House Press (2016)

This book is so much more than a horror story about a mutilation cult. I know that's what horror fans will show up for, right? From cutting off limbs to chopping off fingers and toes, a brotherhood believes that the way to achieve divinity is through the pain and sacrifice of mutilating their bodies. They take a literal interpretation of the Bible where it says, if the hand offends, cut it off. If the eye leads you to sin, pluck it out.

But the actual story centers on the protagonist, Kline, an investigator that caught the cult's attention when he was forced to cut off his own hand and cauterize it himself to save his own life. Two men kidnap him and drive him out to their compound, where they introduce him to one of their leaders. He's given the assignment of investigating a murder. He does not want to get involved but he doesn't have a choice.

Given the dark subject matter, this book is actually quite humorous. Kline is a hardboiled detective type with a take-no-shit attitude and a dry sense of humor. Through his eyes, the absurdity of organized religion gone off the rails is quite entertaining.

The two goons that pick him up are hilarious. The three of them together engage in witty banter throughout the whole story. There are some graphic scenes of violence and horrific descriptions of what these cult members do to themselves, but it's not the vehicle to drive the story. Evenson is a master storyteller, keeping the reader on edge wondering how in the hell Kline is going to untangle himself from this mess without losing too many body parts or his life.

Last Days is an important example of how horror can be cerebral and disturbing while simultaneously poking fun at itself.

THE WINGSPAN OF SEVERED HANDS

BY JOE KOCH (2020)

After calculating probable outcomes for an infinite number of scenarios, a sociologically, emotionally, and mathematically masterful feat accomplished in mere seconds, the weapon decided to pilot itself.

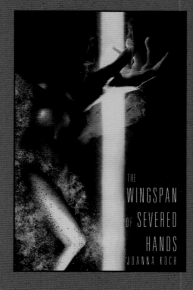

Joe Koch's prose is achingly tragic and beautiful. It's a joy just to spend time with each carefully chosen word, like apples of gold in a setting of silver.

The book opens with a young woman named Adria, trapped in a smothering relationship with her critical, overbearing mother. Interspersed with the linear narrative are provocative, Cronenberg-esque descriptions of everything from shower walls to menstruation, as well as Adria's own body image as if there are two planes of reality: one where Adria is being forced to wed and consummate a marriage and the other a fantastical, gore-tastic fever dream.

Then the point of view shifts to a lab and a conversation between medical personnel that sheds some light on what we've witnessed. The world is in crisis, and this team of scientists are working on an experimental weapon that is supposed to combat a horrible madness sweeping over everything. The fever-dream is actually our reality slipping away from us in our broken minds.

The visuals in this book are like nothing I have ever experienced before in fiction, but remind me of something altogether Lynchian-Cronenbergish-Barkeresque.

The Wingspan of Severed Hands shares a horrifying world of humanity gone off the rails and plumbs the depths of human depravity. I won't claim that I understood everything the author was trying to convey to the audience through the messaging in this book, but I will say that all the chaos, all the emotions, and everything translated that I could tangibly receive, I devoured and stored away in my horror-loving heart.

And now I'm urging you to take this journey.

AT A GLANCE

THEMES: Personal agency, body dysmorphia, rape, creator/creation, bioweapons, the end of civilization, science, mothers and daughters, experiments, scientists, apocalypse, madness, delusion, violence

TONE: Bleak, Blood-Soaked, Brutal, Disturbing, Melancholy, Shocking, Violent

STYLE: Abstract, Brisk Pacing, Cinematic, Clive Barker(ish), Intricately Plotted, Lyrical, Multiple POV

SETTING: N/A

PUBLISHER: Indie/Weirdpunk Books

 # Creepy Kids

Kids can be creepy. Everyone knows this. I'm sure all parents have a story or two about when their children freaked them out with something they did or said. I have a niece that used to see a "bad angel." A childhood friend of mine had a brother that would sleepwalk in the house late at night. One time he was just standing in her closet.

I saw a video where this mom shared footage from their baby monitor. Their little baby sits up suddenly in the middle of the night and stares at the door for several minutes until the end of the video when the baby puts their arms out like someone is about to pick them up. No thanks.

My own son, our eldest, used to stand by our bed, afraid to wake us up, but his presence would trigger me to wake up and see him standing there looking at us. I would freak out, and he would say he was scared and wanted to sleep on the floor. I would tell him every morning, why can't you bring your blankets with you and just sleep on the floor? Why do you have to stare at us like a little weirdo until we wake up and freak out? He wouldn't. That's why. Because kids are

creepy. Nobody knows what's going on in those underdeveloped brains. And because they're children, it's automatically assumed they're innocent. We say that all the time, "innocent children." But what if the child is an instrument of evil? Born bad?

It's unnatural, even counterintuitive to the way our instinct as adults is to protect the little ones and save them from predators. It's hard to imagine a predatory child, and this is why the stories in this section are so horrific.

Creepy kids have a big advantage because it's unexpected. Especially for those of us drawn to coming-of-age horror where the children are often the unlikely heroes, nobody sees it coming when they are the villains.

Ewww, it gives me the willies.

This is a favorite subgenre of horror for me. I love it when horror taps a fear everyone has but nobody wants to admit.

THE LAWS OF THE SKIES

BY GRÉGOIRE COURTOIS (2016)

Before you become an adult, everything is off limits, and, once you become one, you aren't allowed to do anything because you have to be responsible. When in life are we finally free? For good?

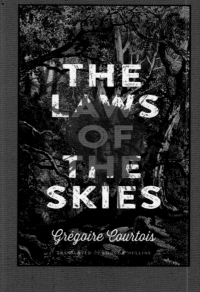

This book is so taboo. Maybe the most taboo book on my list. It is uncomfortable to read, which I think is the point. Horror often forces readers to engage with something we would rather look away from. When I read reviews of this book, it was obvious to me that this French author struck a chord, or better yet, hit a nerve, especially with American readers. It's very telling. Who wants to read a book demonstrating the horrific reality of a child going on a sadistic, murderous rampage?

Certainly, nobody who lives in a society rife with mass shootings. But maybe we should.

Three adults accompany a group of first graders into the woods for a campout. None of them survive the trip. This description is not a spoiler, it's a warning. The author is upfront about what you're headed for right on the first page. Like a demented, twisted version of Agatha Christie's *And Then There Were None*, the characters are picked off one by one. Courtois balances the narrative between different points of view of the adults, the children, and the homicidal maniac—which in this case is a six-year-old boy. It's extremely disturbing. But this isn't the first time I've admired a gruesome depiction of young, sociopathic children exercising their bloodthirst for the first time. We've been here before. It's required reading for most school-age Americans: *The Lord of the Flies* by William Golding. The difference between the two, I think, is that one is a picture of chaos and order apart from authority among the children. *The Laws of the Skies* mirrors a more specific dark corner of humanity: the terrorization of school shootings. So if that's not something you want to wrestle with in your fiction, this one is not for you. If you feel up to the challenge, this is an extremely well-written, unflinching story about stolen innocence.

AT A GLANCE

THEMES: Camping, chaperones, murder, bloodthirst, child sociopaths, innocence, first graders, parents, nature, death, dying, senseless violence

TONE: Bleak, Blood-Soaked, Brutal, Gruesome, Melancholy, Shocking, Violent

STYLE: Brisk Pacing, Cinematic, Lyrical, Multiple POV

SETTING: N/A

PUBLISHER: Indie/Le Quartanier (French); Coach House Books (English translation, 2019)

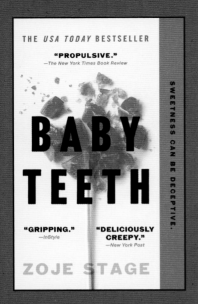

THE *USA TODAY* BESTSELLER

"PROPULSIVE."
—The New York Times Book Review

BABY TEETH

"GRIPPING."
—InStyle

"DELICIOUSLY CREEPY."
—New York Post

ZOJE STAGE

SWEETNESS CAN BE DECEPTIVE.

BABY TEETH

BY ZOJE STAGE (2018)

It was hard to pour endless love into someone who wouldn't love you back. No one could do it forever.

I could not stop reading *Baby Teeth*. Sometimes, I have to live my life and do other things besides reading, but when I didn't have my face buried in this book, I was thinking about it. Essentially, this book is about a family of three in crisis: Suzette, Alex, and their daughter, Hanna, who is non-verbal. Suzette and Hanna have a very unstable, toxic mother-daughter relationship at home while Alex is away for long hours at his job.

The point of view narrative dances back and forth between Suzette and Hanna, while Alex (a pawn in this chess game) is only viewed through their eyes—he is not given a narrative of his own, which I think is utterly fascinating. The most interesting component of the character dynamic is that I don't think any of the three characters are very sympathetic. The reader can observe them from a safe, emotional distance, which I think makes the horror elements very effective. Normally I advocate for characters the reader can invest in so that when they face impossible evil, you're scared for them because you care. In the case of *Baby Teeth*, I just wanted to see how much the drama would escalate. It was a case of being unable to tear my eyes away from a train going off the rails and anticipating how much damage it would do in the end.

AT A GLANCE

THEMES: Family dynamic, domestic drama, psychological horror, manipulation, motherhood, sociopaths, marriage, therapy, anxiety, health issues, behavior disorders

TONE: Disturbing, Intensifying Dread, Shocking, Suspenseful

STYLE: Character-Driven, Cinematic, Leisurely Paced, Multiple POV

SETTING: Pittsburgh, PA

PUBLISHER: Traditional/St. Martin's Press

SUFFER THE CHILDREN

BY CRAIG DILOUIE (2014)

"When it's your child, you don't care about those things. The fluids, smells, crying at all hours of the night." His eyes stung, and he turned to stare out the window. Snow fluttered onto the parking lot. "None of it matters because you love this tiny thing with every atom in your body. The biggest problem every parent has is it goes by too fast. Cherish every minute you have with your child."

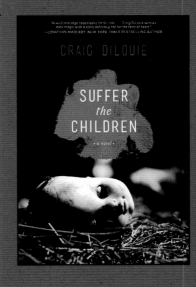

Sometimes the pain of losing a loved one is so traumatizing that people would entertain any kind of relief from the emotional anguish of grief, no matter the consequences.

Suffer the Children takes place during a global pandemic known as Herod's Syndrome, an illness that only affects children and ultimately claims their lives. A whole generation is wiped out. It's a devastating blow to humanity and parents left behind to grieve their collective loss. But the children begin to come back, seemingly unharmed but with an appetite for blood.

I love hybrid horror, and this book mashes up the best of three worlds: zombies, vampires, and creepy children.

The most terrifying aspect of this novel is how the responsibility for morality is left in the hands of desperate parents. Having gone through a global pandemic ourselves in 2020, we know that human beings are not the most reliable species to uphold the tenets of good citizenship when there is a threat to civilization as we know it. All bets are off. It's everyone for themselves. A real fucking nightmare. Some of the parents are relatable in their quest to sustain their family for the foreseeable future ethically, but other parents are self-seeking and turn to questionable methods to look out for their own.

Suffer the Children is a provocative, modern look at the nuclear family during an apocalypse and how the preservation of our own needs could ultimately be the demise of society as a whole.

AT A GLANCE

THEMES: Family, apocalypse, global pandemic, illness, science, vampirism, resurrection, drinking blood, murder, moral compromise, survival, parents, children

TONE: Bleak, Blood-Soaked, Brutal, Menacing, Suspenseful

STYLE: Brisk Pacing, Cinematic, Multiple POV

SETTING: Michigan

PUBLISHER: Traditional/Gallery/Permuted Press

Stephen Graham Jones

Stephen Graham Jones (SGJ) has carved out a niche for himself in horror fiction. A stabby, slashy, bloody niche where his unique voice stands entirely on its own.

I would love to do one of those blind taste tests and have someone give me three stories without a name on them. I bet I could tell you which one he wrote. He leaves fingerprints all over his work. You know you're reading an SGJ story if it's coming-of-age, the main theme is identity, and you feel crushed under the weight of your emotions.

In an interview with *Uncanny Magazine,* SGJ said, "I just figure I am Blackfeet, so every story I tell's going to be Blackfeet." And this is true. Most of his stories are centered on the Native American experience. In 2017, I read my first SGJ book, *Mapping the Interior,* about a twelve-year-old boy who wakes up one night and sees the ghost of his father. Junior lives on a reservation in a small home shared by his widowed mother and his brother, Dino, who is bullied all the time because he has seizures and is developmentally behind. Junior holds his little family together since the passing of his father. This ghost story felt like SGJ was reaching past the page, intentionally trying to hurt my feelings. In about one hundred pages, I was broken. Devastated.

I wanted more.

Mongrels is a book about a family of werewolves isolated from other people like them, so they rely on each other to create a sense of place, culture, and identity as werewolves. The central character, a young man, is learning for himself what it means to be who he is. Boys want to belong. They want to feel important and loved for who they are, and they want to have a place in this world. To be noticed is their goal, but not for being different in a negative way. They want to be different in a way that people celebrate. This book made my heart explode, honestly. From that moment on, SGJ was one of my favorite voices in horror.

Whenever I see SGJ's name on an anthology's Table of Contents, I turn to his story first. His short fiction is everything. I have to mention *Dirtmouth* and *Father, Son, Holy Rabbit.* I can't properly explain how these stories made me feel. They're just so emotional so quickly. How does he do it? I read all of his interviews and listened to him read his work, trying to figure it out, but I've decided it doesn't really matter how he does it, or why, or where. I don't care about the mechanics. I don't need to know anything except when. When do I get my next SGJ fix?

RECOMMENDED TITLES

MAPPING THE INTERIOR (2017)
coming-of-age; ghost story; haunted house

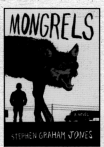

MONGRELS (2016)
coming-of-age; cultural identity; werewolves; outsiders

NIGHT OF THE MANNEQUINS (2020)
coming-of-age; slasher; homage to horror movies

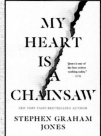

MY HEART IS A CHAINSAW: THE INDIAN LAKE TRILOGY #1 (2021)
coming-of-age; cultural identity; outsiders; slasher; homage to horror movies

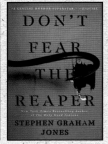

DON'T FEAR THE REAPER: THE INDIAN LAKE TRILOGY #2 (2023)
slasher; manhunt

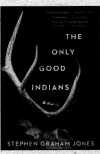

THE ONLY GOOD INDIANS (2020)
revenge; haunted past; cultural identity

THE LAST FINAL GIRL (2012)
screenplay-style narrative; outsiders; slasher

ATTACK OF THE 50 FOOT INDIAN (2020)
satire; social commentary; Native American experience; cultural identity

THE BABYSITTER LIVES (AUDIO, 2022)
haunted house; creepy kids; vengeful spirits

Stephen Graham Jones Recommends: "If I'm to be dispatched in some gnarly fashion, then I can go down smiling because I read Stephen King's *It*, which has all the magic and terror childhood packed in; Gemma Files' *Experimental Film*, for its bright sunshiny horror; and Whitley Strieber's *The Wolfen*, which was the first time I ever got to listen to a werewolf think."

Crime & Investigation

This is the subgenre where real life and fiction intersect the most. The mash-up of crime thrillers and horror. The line of distinction between where crime thrillers end and horror begins is blurry. These unique genre crossovers can be hard to find if you don't know where to look. Thrillers, by obvious definition, "thrill" the audience. They are typically fast paced and action fueled. The escalation of tension as the story progresses induces anxiety and sometimes fear. Primarily, thrillers center around a mystery to solve or a crime that's being investigated.

Horror steps in and makes an appearance when elements indicative of the genre are employed to double down on that fear and anxiety. Those special ingredients added to the mix could include supernatural or paranormal activity, the occult or witchcraft, psychic abilities, cryptids, etc. However, sometimes the horror is just an overall increase in an eerie or spooky atmosphere. Sometimes it's the graphic, violent nature of

the crimes being investigated or the intensity of the criminal. Think about the book *The Silence of the Lambs* by Thomas Harris. Technically, it's a crime investigation of a serial killer shelved under "suspense fiction," but there is nothing but unadulterated horror on those pages. I didn't sleep for a week after I read that book, and I have never parked my car next to a van since.

The most horrific aspect of these books is in their potential to actually happen. Different than the Slashers and Serial Killers subgenre (page 98), crime and investigation horror casts a wide net in order to include mysteries of all kinds: missing people, neighborhood feuds, stalking, kidnapping, and other horrible, heinous crimes.

The monstrosities of true crime inspiring fictional horrors make for an exhilarating reading experience. These books are the best of both worlds.

NUMBER ONE FAN

BY MEG ELISON (2022)

He saw the tight-knit knot of celebrity writers at its center. He saw the way they tweeted at one another, the photos of them drinking together at convention hotels. Their blurbs on one another's books, their chummy sharing of links, and boosting of good news. He felt like he was pressing his nose against a warm window and he was desperate to come in out of the cold. He would be one of them one day.

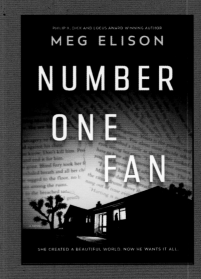

Yes, this is the story of a fan kidnapping their favorite writer, but no, it's not trying to be Stephen King's *Misery*. King's story is more of a "spider trapped a fly" scenario, whereas Elison's is a twist on classic obsessive stalker tropes like *YOU* by Caroline Kepnes: more horror, less thriller.

The way that this story is so fucking plausible is the scariest part about it. It's a cautionary tale to women to *never* let our guard down for even a single, solitary moment, and to consider how much of ourselves we reveal on the internet for any stranger to know.

Bestselling author Eli Grey finds herself in a basement of an unhinged fan. The only person that might notice she's missing is her assistant, but that could take days. Eli must endure the worst possible situation without even a shred of hope that anyone is looking for her.

Meg Elison utilizes our modern world of Uber, social media, cell phones, emails, and countless other ways strangers can access and exploit someone's personal life and creates a real nightmare for readers. An important, modern work of horror, this book exposes how truly vulnerable we are in the wrong hands.

Readers should know going into this that none of it is an exaggeration. If anything, Meg Elison pulled some punches because "Book Twitter" is a whole fucking vibe. There must be hundreds, if not thousands, of writers who experience jealous feelings daily as they keep tabs on the hourly highlight reel from their friends and colleagues online. When you're on the outside, looking in, how easily that could turn into something sociopathic and weird makes *Number One Fan* not at all outside the realm of possibility. Which is creepy and gross and scary as hell.

AT A GLANCE

THEMES: Writers, publishing, fandom, fan fiction, kidnapping, torture, fame, jealousy, delusion, outcasts, social media

TONE: Bleak, Blood-Soaked, Brutal, Menacing, Shocking, Suspenseful, Violent

STYLE: Brisk Pacing, Character-Driven

SETTING: California City, CA

PUBLISHER: Traditional/Mira Books

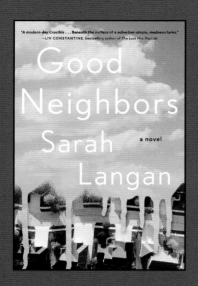

"A modern-day Crucible . . . Beneath the surface of a suburban utopia, madness lurks."
—LIV CONSTANTINE, bestselling author of *The Last Mrs. Parrish*

Good Neighbors

Sarah Langan

a novel

AT A GLANCE

GRL PWR

THEMES: Neighbors, community, gossip, sinkholes, upper middle class, secrets, lies, suburbia, power dynamics

TONE: Disturbing, Humorous, Intensifying Dread, Menacing, Shocking, Suspenseful, Violent

STYLE: Brisk Pacing, Character-Driven, Critically Acclaimed, Intricately Plotted, Multiple POV

SETTING: N/A

PUBLISHER: Traditional/Atria Books

GOOD NEIGHBORS

BY SARAH LANGAN (2021)

Like, if your life isn't perfect, you keep your mouth shut and don't talk about it until it is perfect, and then you brag.

There were times when I was reading this book with my eyes wide with surprise and my mouth dropped open. What happens on these pages is unbelievable, and yet, we see examples of people going off the rails every day.

Sarah Langan's *Good Neighbors* wraps the reader up in a heavy blanket of tension as the narrative establishes a dangerous power dynamic among neighbors in American suburbia. The reigning matriarchal family on Maple Street feels threatened when a new family moves in. A sinkhole opens up and is a catalyst for all hell breaking loose when something happens to one of the kids. An absolutely explosive game of "their word against ours" turns the neighborhood into a warzone where every family is expected to choose a side. There is clearly only one side that is "right."

Setting this book just a few years out into the future, Langan is able to shed some light on issues we're all struggling with today and reveal what they would look like, unresolved, in a few years' time.

This reading experience feels like a deep dive into a true crime story. It's like something one finds in the news or listens to on a podcast, and it just feels so unbelievable what people will do to each other and how a small misunderstanding can escalate into full-blown violence. *Good Neighbors* is a master class in building tension chapter after chapter; readers will absolutely experience tangible anxiety and other emotions that make your heart race.

Sarah Langan's engrossing storytelling style keeps readers locked on the page until the end, making it one of the best modern character-driven stories of our time.

COYOTE SONGS

BY GABINO IGLESIAS (2018)

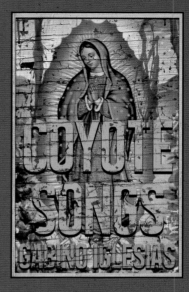

However, the man was wrong. It wasn't a hundred coyotes with bullhorns howling at once and it wasn't the Devil himself. The things that had screamed that night was the soul of a shattered, hurt mother facing the loss of everything she loved, and that is something even the Devil should fear.

Coyote Songs begins with blood.

And pain.

Gabino introduces readers to the storytellers: Pedrito, Alma, The Mother, The Coyote, Jamie, and The Bruja. Their tales will leave an impression on your heart like a tattoo. The way that Gabino Iglesias can float you through an exotic blend of genres without a misstep is nothing short of a fairytale. As I say that, it reminds me of the way the language in this book fluidly transitions from English to Spanish, and I barely even noticed. I Google translated some sentences or a few words, but sometimes, I think my mind translated it for me through some kind of barrio noir magic.

Coyote Songs is not a linear story. There are several stories the reader is following, each chapter a vignette, a singular tile set in a larger piece of work to create a whole picture, like a mosaic. The stories tell the different experiences of Mexican culture specifically as they relate to tragedies like immigration, human trafficking, and racism. There are some very heavy feminine voices coupled with the voices of children— it's refreshing to find marginalized people groups at the center of a powerful and impactful book like this one.

Having grown up experiencing Mexican culture on my grandpa's side of the family, I'm familiar with a lot of the matriarchal and super-stitious threads I found pulling all of these stories together in the beautiful, yet haunting tapestry that is *Coyote Songs*.

AT A GLANCE

THEMES: Superstitions, Latin culture, gods and goddesses, magic, folklore, human trafficking, racism, immigrants, religion, revenge, grief, myths and legends

TONE: Bleak, Brutal, Disturbing, Lyrical, Menacing

STYLE: Cinematic, Multiple POV, Vignettes

SETTING: Mexico/Mexican border/Texas

PUBLISHER: Traditional/ Broken River Books

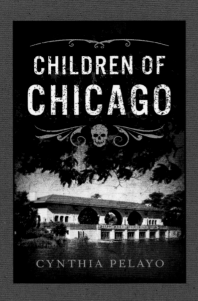

CHILDREN OF CHICAGO

BY CYNTHIA PELAYO (2021)

Chicago was plagued with hundreds and hundreds of unsolved murders and missing persons cases. Lauren knew this was her purgatory, her reason for living to find them and set this right.

Where are my crime-noir thriller book lovers? You can have your horror and your thriller-junkie vibes in one book. *Children of Chicago* is a retelling of the "Pied Piper of Hamelin" folklore tale.

Lauren Medina is a detective working the streets of Chicago. Her mother's disappearance and her sister's unsolved murder case are the driving force behind Lauren's passion to keep children safe in her neighborhood. Despite all her dutiful diligence, children are being hunted by a killer known as the Pied Piper.

The authorities are unwilling to give credence to this generational urban legend, scolding Lauren for indulging in superstitions. But Lauren has her secrets: her hidden connection to her sister's death and a promise made to a killer. As the danger intensifies, a battle for truth and justice wages war inside Lauren's soul. She throws herself into the investigation, bringing her closer and closer to the answers she's not sure she wants to face.

This is a page-turning binge-read for folks who love to get immersed in a good ol' fashioned police procedural but also enjoy all the grisly details horror stories have to offer.

AT A GLANCE

THEMES: Missing and/ or murdered children, city life, serial killers, police investigations, women detectives, urban myths/ legends, fairytales, trauma

TONE: Dark, Gruesome, Melancholy, Menacing, Suspenseful, Violent

STYLE: Brisk Pacing, Cinematic

SETTING: Chicago, Illinois

PUBLISHER: Traditional/Polis Books

BROKEN MONSTERS

BY LAUREN BEUKES (2014)

Everyone lives three versions of themselves; a public life, a private life and a secret life.

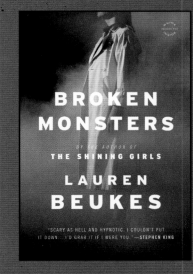

Broken Monsters by Lauren Beukes is horror with police procedural and crime investigation elements, so it's shelved with thrillers. But trust me, this one is scary as fuck.

A serial killer operating in the Detroit area is curating his crime scenes by fusing his victim's bodies with dead animals. Beukes uses multiple points of view to tell one gruesome story from different vantage points, giving the reader a vibrant, well-rounded picture of graphic violence and how it affects a community in varying degrees.

Beukes is a master at building a multifaceted narrative, leading readers to formulate their own theories and assign motive to certain key players. But no matter how good you think your sleuthing skills are, Beukes is several steps ahead of you—this I know for certain. *Broken Monsters* truly has one of the most compelling storylines you'll ever run across leaning into both the natural and the supernatural. To manage early expectations, understand that it will take a minute to keep all of the characters straight. The narrative is going to feel like it's bouncing around a lot, but stick with it. This is like a 1,000-piece literary puzzle where you, the reader, are sorting pieces and putting together the framework for awhile, then suddenly . . . everything starts coming together. The payoff is huge.

AT A GLANCE

THEMES: Artists, sociopaths, psychopaths, single mothers, teenage girls, work/home life balance, investigations, murder, serial killers, journalism, fame, unhoused people, digital age

TONE: Bleak, Blood-Soaked, Brutal, Intensifying Dread, Menacing, Suspenseful

STYLE: Brisk Pacing, Character-Driven, Cinematic, Intricately Plotted, Multiple POV

SETTING: Detroit

PUBLISHER: Traditional/ Mulholland Books

A Secret Language Only We Can Speak: The Comfort of Queer Horror

BY ERIC LAROCCA

When I first connected with Sadie Hartmann (or "Mother Horror" as she's affectionately referred to by friends and fans alike), I was deep in the trenches of the indie/small press horror community and preparing for the release of my debut Weirdpunk Books novella, *Things Have Gotten Worse Since We Last Spoke*. Of course, I knew the cover artwork (painted by Swedish artist Kim Jakobsson) was provocative, and I knew for certain that the title was alluring; however, I scarcely expected the success I would see from that particular book. The publishing industry opened its doors to me, and I found myself navigating unfamiliar territory as I came under heavy scrutiny from readers. Not only did I fall under heavy examination, but the indie horror community saw a surge in popularity with other small press titles gaining attention and notoriety.

As I write this piece, I have had the privilege of seeing a collection of my short fiction (*Things Have Gotten Worse Since We Last Spoke and Other Misfortunes*) be published by Titan Books. In the coming months, I will focus my attention on my next Titan collection titled *The Trees Grew Because I Bled There: Collected Stories*. It's, of course, very daunting to make the leap from small press to a traditional publishing house, especially one as reputable and with a wildly impressive catalog as Titan Books. That said, more and more, I see the weird/eclectic/outlandishly bizarre sensibilities of some of the small presses leeching into the traditional publishing houses. Moreover, I see writers from marginalized communities being plucked from obscurity and rightfully lauded for their talent, fearlessness, and verve.

There are countless authors who come to mind; however, two of the most recent examples of queer horror authors operating in the small press space and then jumping to a larger imprint would be Gretchen Felker-Martin (author of *Manhunt*) and Alison Rumfitt (author of *Tell Me I'm Worthless*). Both authors saw success in the indie space before inking substantial contracts with a larger imprint. In fact, Alison's brilliant novel, *Tell Me I'm Worthless*, was originally published by a small UK press, and when it garnered considerable attention online, Tor Nightfire immediately took an interest and purchased US rights. To me, this says two things: (1) The big publishing houses are diligently watching the indie/small press horror space, and (2) there is a significant demand for the complexities and the dynamics at play in queer horror.

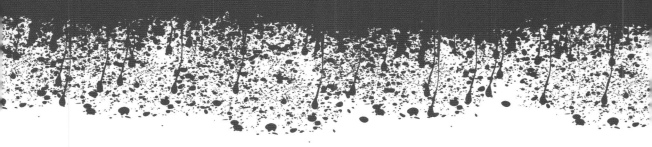

Of course, some might scoff when they hear the term "queer horror." Others might condemn it and turn up their nose. Whether you are receptive to the notion or not, the horror genre is an inherently queer space. Not only have queer characters existed (as carefully coded figures) in films since the Pre-Code era (*The Old Dark House, The Bride of Frankenstein*), but the genre also seems to inherently attract queer readers and viewers simply because horror is a joyful celebration of "the other." As queer people, we intrinsically are "the other." We are forever on the outside. We are not considered "normal" by conventional, cisgender, and heterosexual standards.

Although horror has long been accused of being a misogynistic and homophobic genre, we are seeing a tremendous shift in the stories being told. It's especially apparent in the small press sphere with new titles being released on a weekly basis that effectively challenge some of the harmful stereotypes set forth by our predecessors. Moreover, some of these titles written by marginalized voices are attracting considerable attention on platforms like Instagram and TikTok. Because of the accessibility to "go viral" on some of these platforms, many books that would have otherwise gone unnoticed are having their moment and seeing remarkable success.

As I look forward to seeing the release of my second traditionally published book, I am very mindful of the demand for disturbing, "in-your-face" queer horror. Of course, there have been countless authors that have operated in this space. I think of writers like Clive Barker or Poppy Z. Brite. It's heartening to see such a warm reception for dark, complex queer characters in horror fiction. More importantly, it's very encouraging to see just how devoted the readers are and how they seek out works that are transgressive and boundary-pushing.

Whenever I read work by my colleagues—queer-specific work that challenges me, upsets me, disturbs me—I find myself feeling less alone. For so long, I existed on an island inside my mind. I would see others in the distance, but I was never close enough to touch them. It wasn't until I started reading blatantly queer horror fiction (books like *Red X* by David Demchuk or *Skin* by Kathe Koja) that I found my true self. I found my soul. I found my voice as a writer.

A very kind reader once wrote me a detailed "fan letter" about one of my books. I'll never forget when they wrote: "Sometimes we need to read something awful in order to feel better." That's exactly how I feel when I read disturbing, transgressive books by queer authors. Often, it feels like a secret language that only we can speak. Perhaps one day you'll join us . . .

Eric LaRocca (*he/they*) is the Splatterpunk Award-winning and Bram Stoker Award-nominated author of the viral sensation, *Things Have Gotten Worse Since We Last Spoke*. He can often be found roaming the streets of his home city, Boston, MA, for inspiration.

NATURAL ORDER HORROR

WE LIVE IN A WORLD THAT is trying to kill us. We are the weakest link. Take away our technology and our weapons and what do we have? Nothing. Our teeth aren't sharp, we don't have claws, and most of us can't outrun anything that has four legs. We can't even hide. Nobody is naturally camouflaged, and we're very noisy.

Nature is terrifying. I try my very best to stay out of it, but my family does require my participation in certain outdoor family outings, so I reluctantly have to be a brave adventurer and try to enjoy the beauty of our world while simultaneously ignoring the brutality. If you're like me and want to live a long life and not get murdered or fall off a cliff, make some guidelines for safe living. In the meantime, you can borrow some of mine:

● The ocean is enjoyable at a safe distance from the shore. I will not willingly put my body in the ocean. *Jaws* is real. The only way to never encounter a shark is to stay out of the ocean. Period. Besides, all sea animals are scary.

● I will not hike off-trail or spend the night outside. I have a comfy bed indoors that is designed for sleeping and safety while I am vulnerable, so I will not get inside a cold bag with a zipper in a makeshift house with fabric walls to protect me from predators or insects. That's ridiculous.

● Spiders are a major issue for me, so outdoor activities are considered based on the probability of encountering spiders in their natural habitat. A jungle tour in Mexico was immediately canceled upon discovering the hideous species of spider that lives there.

● Exploring caves is out of the question. There are well over a hundred reasons caves are problematic. I won't bore you with all of them, but here are the major ones: Darkness, bats, bugs, tight spaces, sharp rocks, animals, subterranean cannibals, an alien species we haven't discovered yet, mold or spores, tripping, falling, and so on.

● Humans in large quantities are awful. I avoid crowds at all costs. Disneyland might be the happiest place on Earth, but it's the last place I want to be in a crisis. If the zombie apocalypse begins, where do you want to be? Disneyland? Certainly not. And think of the germs present when you're among crowds of humans. We're a very dirty, germy species.

Five important rules to live by. I have more, obviously, but this is because I'm a scaredy cat who reads a lot of horror. The more horror books you read, the wiser you become.

Included in this section are books about natural disasters, apocalyptic survival, killer wildlife and plants, and probably every fear or phobia you might have represented in a horror book.

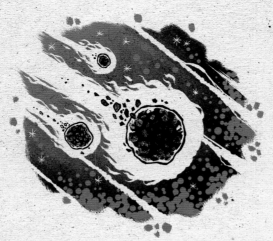

Apocalyptic, Dystopian & Sci-Fi

Human beings are obsessed with our own demise. It's something we fantasize about all the time. I think it's funny and rather endearing. All those summer blockbuster movies about natural global disasters, plagues, alien invasions, and the zombie apocalypse. We love to tell the story of how most of the world's population is wiped out so small groups of survivors must endure many hardships in order to sustain human life on earth.

We are endlessly fascinated and entertained by this subject! And it's not just epic movies, it's epic books too. Some of these books are door stoppers, weighing in at seven-hundred plus pages. Apocalyptic fiction gives a detailed account of how everything goes to shit. It starts at the beginning and takes us all the way through life as we know it coming to a full stop. We love it! It doesn't even matter that nobody brings anything new to the table. We like the same old tropes.

Sometimes I imagine an alien species taking a close look at us while we pack ourselves into a dark theater and watch other humans on a screen who have spent copious amounts of money and time on this big production just to show us this tale of a time when aliens have come in fancy spaceships to destroy all our cities and kill us all. And we sit there with our snacks and our soda and just enjoy every minute of it.

How ridiculous and cute.

Some of us tell others that our favorite Stephen King book is *The Stand*. You know, this horrible disease that kills a bunch of people and the remaining people form these camps of good and evil and fight each other? Cool, cool. It hits a little differently post-COVID; fifty years later, *The Stand* isn't that far flung from reality. Scary. Or *The Handmaid's Tale* by Margaret Atwood? Also hitting close to home.

How is this subgenre so popular when we're actually living it out in reality? I don't know the answer, but I do know that I'm one of them. I love a good story about everyone dying. My guess is you'll like it too, so here are my choices for the ones you should read before you're annihilated.

ZONE ONE

BY COLSON WHITEHEAD (2011)

You're still the person you were before the plague, you tell yourself, even though you're running for dear life through the parking lot of some shitty mall, being chased by a gang of monsters.

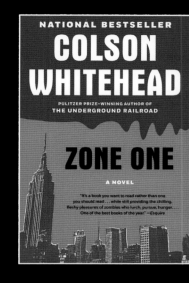

I'm a hard sell when it comes to zombie books, so if I ever recommend one, you know it's good. It's mainly the tropes. I find them to be too repetitive across the board, you know? If you've read one zombie book, you've read them all.

With a few exceptions.

Colson Whitehead's *Zone One* to be exact. This is quintessential horror, first and foremost. It's pitch perfect from start to finish—basically one weekend in the life of a guy nicknamed Mark Spitz. He's part of a team of "Sweepers," armed forces who systematically move through the city and clean up after the military has mostly eliminated the zombie population.

The narrative alternates between flashbacks and detailing real-time events through Mark Spitz's point of view. Society is ravaged by the plague. People are compartmentalized into their own, small groups: the military, small bands of survivors, Sweepers, and the dead ("stragglers" that are fixed to one spot and easy to pick off or "skels" that are dangerous and mobile).

All living people suffer from PASD, Post Apocalyptic Stress Disorder. Relatable in the times after 2020, actually. Whitehead spins a fantastic yarn. It's appropriately bleak considering the circumstances, but there are these beautiful moments of normal life that shine through and break your heart. This story is peppered with social commentary, wisdom on humanity, and that magical way that people come together in dark, dark times.

I'm baffled as to why this isn't a movie or why other zombie books were adapted over this one because . . . This. Is. The. One.

AT A GLANCE

THEMES: Zombie apocalypse, survival, humanity, human psychology, trauma, friendship, coping in a crisis, suicide, satire, dark humor

TONE: Bleak, Disturbing, Gruesome, Humorous, Intensifying Dread, Melancholy, Violent

STYLE: Brisk Pacing, Cinematic, Intricately Plotted

SETTING: NYC, New York

PUBLISHER: Traditional/Doubleday Books

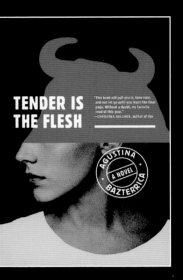

TENDER IS THE FLESH

BY AUGUSTINA BAZTERRICA (2017)

After all, since the world began, we've been eating each other. If not symbolically, then we've been literally gorging on each other. The Transition has enabled us to be less hypocritical.

Sometime in the not-too-distant future in a dystopian world not unlike our own, a virus has rendered all animals too toxic for humans to consume or even domesticate. There are no pets. Humans are not able to enjoy the company of animals, and eating animals or animal byproducts is a luxury of the past.

Eventually, mankind finds a solution in breeding humans for consumption. The understated violence of this book is so utterly disarming that it takes a minute to find your footing.

The story centers around a "special meat" processing plant manager named Marcos Tejo. Marcos is a strange character. He moves through life almost totally devoid of emotion. He and his wife are estranged after the death of their son. He has a strained, complicated relationship with his ailing father, and he works at this factory where humans are bred and slaughtered for food.

Bazterrica unravels the tale with unflinching precision; graphic details feel clinical in their delivery. The overall tone is cold and calculating; the words are like a scalpel's edge. The lack of emotion is arresting at first, but soon, it becomes familiar. The reader is forced to wrestle with crimes against humanity carried out in this morally bankrupt, emotionally sterile environment, which makes *Tender is the Flesh* one of the most thought-provoking novels I've ever read. I felt conflicted about even enjoying my reading experience. The ending lingers in my mind still today.

AT A GLANCE

THEMES: Humanity, morality, human relationships to food, the animal kingdom, society, cannibalism, complacency, viral pandemic, emotional desensitization

TONE: Bleak, Dark, Disturbing, Gruesome, Melancholy, Shocking, Violent

STYLE: Brisk Pacing, Intricately Plotted

SETTING: A dystopian world in a Latin country

PUBLISHER: Traditional/ Alfaguara (Spanish; Castilian); Scribner (English translation, 2020)

RING SHOUT

BY P. DJÈLÍ CLARK (2020)

*I ain't no scared girl no more. I hunt monsters—
they don't hunt me. So now I'm about to
do something real brave or stupid.*

Ring Shout was my favorite book in 2020 and is in my top ten books of all time. I got an advance reading copy on my Kindle, and I'm recommending readers buy both the e-book and the physical editions because the e-reading experience is so rich. P. Djèlí Clark is an academic historian. He infuses his vast knowledge and research into his speculative fiction, so as you read *Ring Shout* on the e-reader, you can highlight specific sections and learn as you go. It's an interactive way to engage with the historical elements of this story that I felt enhanced the experience. I felt like I was getting a solid education on Black history while also enjoying a dark fantasy tale and seriously scary horror.

In 1920s Georgia, Maryse Boudreaux knows everything there is to know about human monsters involved in the KKK, as well as the supernatural demon monsters Maryse and her friends call Ku Kluxes, who are determined to destroy humanity. Maryse is a "chosen one" hero. At some point in her life, she was singled out as a protector and given a magic sword. The sword embodies the war cries and testimonies of martyrs and fighters who have gone before her on similar quests for justice against oppression. Things get tricky for Maryse when a new leader shows up on the scene, amplifying an even darker message of hate.

The stakes are so high in this story, and the evil is overwhelmingly powerful and scary. Clark moves this tale along at a breakneck pace with edge-of-your-seat suspense. Every chapter ends with a fresh urgency to continue. I want more for this universe. I hope P. Djèlí Clark has more Maryse Boudreaux stories to tell because, even though *Ring Shout* felt like a complete book and I was not found wanting, I could see the potential for Maryse's journey to either continue into more quests and adventures or for the author to write some of the backstories to some of the unusual, unique characters.

AT A GLANCE

THEMES: African American history, enslavement, racism, hatred, humanity, monsters, demons, KKK, empowerment psychic ability, violence, folklore, strong female warriors

TONE: Dark, Disturbing, Intensifying Dread, Menacing, Shocking, Suspenseful, Violent

STYLE: Brisk Pacing, Character-Driven, Cinematic, Intricately Plotted

SETTING: 1920s Georgia

PUBLISHER: Traditional/ Tordotcom

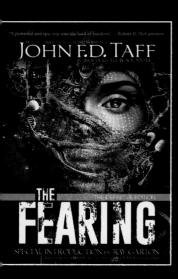

THE FEARING: THE DEFINITIVE EDITION

BY JOHN F. D. TAFF (2021)

"Fear. Simple as that. Fear. There's so much of it that it's gumming up the system, obstructing the world from its true purpose." "Which is?" "Light. Love. Advancement. Peace. Whichever you'd like, they're all faces of the same thing. Just as hatred, anger and violence are faces of fear."

Did you know that they call John F. D. Taff "The King of Pain"? It's true. They do. *The Fearing* is the perfect example of why he holds this title. It has everything to do with how Taff lovingly, intentionally, and expertly leads his audience into character-driven horror where you will rip your own heart out and offer it, willingly, to the King of Pain so he can destroy it. Doesn't that sound fun?

Lucky for you, *The Fearing* is four books collected in a single volume now for your convenience, and you don't have to wait between books for your next fix. *The Fearing* is about a global phenomenon that's causing everyone's worst fears to become a reality. Taff brings together some unlikely heroes, following their journey of survival in multiple points of view for every chapter. Horror fans have enjoyed this setup in prior iconic apocalyptic books, like Stephen King's *The Stand* and Robert McCammon's *Swan Song*. Taff's offering is a worthy asset to the tradition.

There are several traveling groups navigating the nightmarish landscape of *The Fearing*: a group of teens, a bus full of aging grown-ups, the antagonist, and a few more sets of characters. Taff is definitely aiming for readers' hearts as he exposes his characters to us through meaningful dialogue, internal struggles, and physical/mental anguish.

The emotional investment in these characters' lives is what makes the horror so damn real. If you love apocalyptic, large-scale horror, this one's for you.

THE SILENCE

BY TIM LEBBON (2015)

Stay quiet, stay alive.

Forget everything you know about alien predators that hunt by sound. Throw out the movies *A Quiet Place I & II*, as well as the Netflix adaptation of this book. Just cleanse your brain of those cinematic experiences and biases before you jump into Tim Lebbon's original source material, *The Silence*.

In a deep subterranean environment, live creatures have been unable to reach the surface of our planet, until now. Hunting their prey by sound, the creatures escape their underground lair and become a new apex predator. Lebbon zeroes in on one family trying to survive this hostile takeover by relying on Ally, a fourteen-year-old who is deaf, to help them navigate their way to safety as quietly as they can.

This is true character-driven horror with heart. Lebbon draws on our empathy and emotions as we journey with a father and his kids through some heart-pounding situations, escaping creatures called Vesps and monsters of the human variety.

What makes the story unique is how the characters must communicate in non-verbal ways. Ally and her family know sign language, but they also develop a language of facial expressions, lip reading, and small gestures to use in very tense circumstances.

Even though trying times are bleak and seem hopeless, Lebbon keeps his characters pressing on under the banner of love. At the end of the day, no matter what, all we have is each other, and that is one of my favorite horror themes.

AT A GLANCE

THEMES: Survival, creature feature, plague, monsters, hearing impaired, fathers and daughters, family, love, living with disabilities, sacrifice, perseverance

TONE: Intensifying Dread, Melancholy, Suspenseful

STYLE: Brisk Pacing, Character-Driven, Cinematic, Intricately Plotted, Multiple POV

SETTING: Rural Scotland

PUBLISHER: Traditional/Titan Books

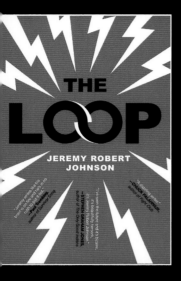

THE LOOP

BY JEREMY ROBERT JOHNSON (2020)

This isn't fair. I'm only a kid. A fucking kid. Holy shit. We're all going to die. Everyone.

Cue some strange intro music, like the eerie riffs from *X-Files* or the digital notes of that synthesized melody from *Stranger Things,* and settle into this binge-worthy genre mashup. Best known for his bizarro-horror style and flavor, Jeremy Robert Johnson is an unexpected hero in the coming-of-age, conspiracy-thriller, zombie-apocalypse genre. (His short story collection, *Entropy in Bloom,* is a must.)

If you don't have to eat, sleep, or live your life, you will easily read this book in one sitting. If you do have a life and must place a bookmark now and then, prepare to think about this book even when you're not reading it.

A small town in Oregon becomes the epicenter for some unusual, violent activity among the townspeople due to a failed science experiment. A group of teenage oddballs and outcasts led by Lucy and her friend Bucket, the only two "brown kids" at the Turner Falls high school, must survive the next twenty-four hours and save the world by preventing the outbreak from spreading beyond the town's borders.

One of my favorite aspects of Johnson's writing is the way everything is stylistically cinematic to read, like a cult classic from the late '80s to mid-'90s. This book is a vibe.

AT A GLANCE

THEMES: Young adults, high school, evil corporations, conspiracy theories, small town horror, marginalized experience, outcasts, white privilege, classism, survival, zombies, science experiments

TONE: Dark, Eerie, Humorous, Intensifying Dread, Menacing, Suspenseful, Violent

STYLE: Brisk Pacing, Character-Driven

SETTING: Oregon

PUBLISHER: Traditional/Saga Press

Want More Epic Apocalypse Books?

WANDERERS & WAYWARD BY CHUCK WENDIG
STATION ELEVEN BY EMILY ST. JOHN MANDEL
SURVIVAL SONG BY PAUL TREMBLAY
SWAN SONG BY ROBERT MCCAMMON
THE FIREMAN BY JOE HILL
THE ROAD BY CORMAC MCCARTHY
THE PASSAGE BY JUSTIN CRONIN
PARABLE OF THE SOWER BY OCTAVIA BUTLER

101 HORROR BOOKS TO READ BEFORE YOU'RE MURDERED

RED HANDS

BY CHRISTOPHER GOLDEN (2020)

*"Sentient, malevolent disease," Rue said quietly.
"That's not possible."*

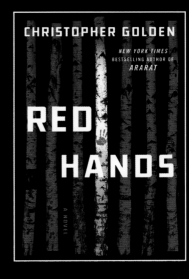

I cannot stress to readers enough how utterly compulsive this book feels while you're reading it. The energy is masterfully held in tension throughout the entire development of the story. Golden never relaxes that sense of urgency he manufactures right in the beginning. This is book three in the Ben Walker series, but I promise this reads like a standalone novel and you won't miss out on anything except maybe built-in love for recurring characters.

Golden wastes zero time building up to the action as chapter one explodes with chaos. I was reminded of the first chapter of *Cell* by Stephen King where the reader is an observer of a series of catastrophic events and tragedy right on page one.

In *Red Hands*, we meet Maeve Sinclair, who is enjoying a 4th of July parade in a small town with her family when suddenly, a car comes out of nowhere and drives into the crowd at random. As she watches friends and family suffer under the wheels of a homicidal maniac, a fire burns within her and she risks everything to confront the driver as he emerges from his car. Everyone this man touches dies.

Maeve hits the murderer with a baseball bat, and when he dies, something happens to Maeve. In an unexpected turn of events, she flees the scene to hide out in the nearby woods. All of this compelling and shocking action happens in the first scene!

"Weird shit" expert Ben Walker is called in to investigate a strange phenomenon known as the "Death Touch." He works for an organization that pursues scientific abnormalities and occurrences before the "wrong people" catch wind of them to militarize or weaponize them. Walker comes alive on the page as a fully fleshed-out human being that I immediately fell in love with. He's whip-crack smart, both intellectually and in wit and sarcasm. I also fell in love with Maeve and felt genuine concern and heartache for her safety. Of course, balancing out these two likable characters are the people hunting Maeve to exploit her and her new ability, making this one of the most compelling supernatural thrillers I've had the pleasure of reading in a long, long time.

AT A GLANCE

THEMES: Biological weapons, secret government agencies, communicable diseases, death, strange phenomena, weird science

TONE: Dark, Intensifying Dread, Menacing, Suspenseful

STYLE: Brisk Pacing, Character-Driven, Cinematic, Intricately Plotted, Stephen King(ish)

SETTING: New Hampshire

PUBLISHER: Traditional/St. Martin's Press

Alma Katsu

I think I should start with how Alma Katsu is an actual badass. Before she began her career as a bestselling novelist, she worked as a senior intelligence analyst for several federal agencies. I believe that experience translates through her storytelling. I just imagine that all the skills and knowledge it would require to advise government officials on issues of national security are the same skills and knowledge Alma puts to work developing fictional stories against historical backdrops.

The Hunger balances a historical depiction of the Donner Party traveling on the Oregon Trail toward California. As a native Californian, this story is ingrained in my DNA. All California kids know the tragedy of the Donner Party (who had to eat dead people to stay alive), and we all learned computer skills by playing floppy-disk editions of *Oregon Trail* on our fancy Macintosh computers. Alma takes an already horrific story and infuses it with supernatural elements. The characters, especially the women, come to life on the page through scenes of interpersonal drama between the travelers as they try to navigate the harsh landscape, the threat of starvation, and something hunting them out there in the wilderness. It's ridiculously compelling. Plan on not doing anything else once you start it.

Leaning into her passion for history once again, Alma Katsu gave readers *The Deep* in early 2020, right when COVID hit and we all got our first stay-at-home orders. I'm sure this was a very unfortunate time for launching a book, but for readers stuck at home under extreme duress and uncertainty, it was a lifesaver. A tale surrounding the sinkings of the *Titanic* and its sister ship, the *Britannic*, I was mesmerized by Katsu's storytelling and utterly immersed in the intricately plotted dual timelines and multiple points of view. Horror elements are expertly infused into the rich, historical setting, peppered with themes of grief, shame, romance, and a whole plethora of feelings that come along with survival stories.

Photo by Suzette Niess.

Perhaps my favorite Alma Katsu book (hard to choose) is her Bram Stoker Award®-nominated novel, *The Fervor*, a supernatural twist on the very real historical hardships endured during World War II in Japanese American internment camps. The attack on Pearl Harbor generated Asian hate, something that hits hard for readers so soon after the hate we witnessed in the last two years. This book explores the emotional and psychological turmoil of people suffering under the weight of racial tension, government propaganda and rhetoric, and the unrelenting threat of white supremacy.

The greatest joy of reading is living other lives and traveling to unfamiliar worlds. Katsu doubles down on that joy by immersing readers in our past. I always come away from her books feeling like I've learned something.

RECOMMENDED TITLES

THE HUNGER (2018)	THE DEEP (2020)	THE FERVOR (2022)	THE WEHRWOLF (2022)	RED WIDOW (2021)	THE TAKER SERIES (2011-2013)
historical; supernatural predators; The Donner Party	*historical; paranormal; The Titanic*	*historical; Japanese Americans; World War II*	*historical; Nazi Germany; World War II; human and supernatural monsters*	*spy thriller; investigative mystery; Putin's Russia; series*	*paranormal romance; dark fantasy; trilogy*

Alma Katsu Recommends: "*The Little Stranger* by Sarah Waters. The most believable ghost story ever. *The Only Good Indians* by Stephen Graham Jones. *The Last House on Needless Street* by Catriona Ward. Ward has the perfect voice for horror."

Eco-Horror

The other day I tripped out on how insignificant I am in relation to the big picture. I imagined myself sitting in my house typing up this book, and then I zoomed out and saw my city, the state of Washington, the whole United States, Earth—which is just this rock floating in some solar system in this infinite galaxy with a bazillion other floating rocks in the vast, black, void of endless space.

Think about how vulnerable we are in this context. At any moment, a bigger rock can come rocketing toward us and take the whole thing out. Boom! Gone. The ocean could swallow all the cities on the coastlines. A tornado could suck up your house and plop it down in Oz. A volcano could erupt and bury everything in its path under a fiery torrent of molten sludge from the Earth's core. A tree could fall through your house and block the only door to get in or out of the bathroom your family gathered in during a storm. Your ship could get stuck in a frozen ocean in the middle of nowhere. You could find yourself at the bottom of the ocean and discover you're not alone down there.

What if you and your friends find yourselves lost in a jungle where the vines are evil and want to kill everyone? Or maybe an alien species decides to take up residence here and we don't know anything about the flora and fauna, so we have to explore it ourselves to determine if it's hostile (It is. It's very hostile).

We are at the mercy of our natural environment, and nobody is coming to save us. That makes for great horror. I picked these next books so that, upon finishing them, you will question how you were ever able to exist on this planet without thinking of your own mortality at least every hour of every day. Horror serves as a way to reorient our thinking so that we are always living in fear. As we should be.

WE NEED TO DO SOMETHING

BY MAX BOOTH III (2020)

Residential bathrooms like this are built for one person at a time. One door, a shower/tub combo, a toilet, a tiny trash can, a sink and mirror. All of us crammed in here together, the room has never felt so small. The reality of its size burns into my skull.

Imagine a rubber band held tight to its snapping point and a sharp edge applying the tiniest amount of pressure. That's how I felt reading this story, like I was turning the crank of a jack-in-the-box pop-up toy. Which maybe doesn't sound so bad, except what if I told you that once the Jack pops up, he's going to stab you in the feelings over and over again until everything goes really dark? That's this book.

A family runs into their bathroom to take shelter during a violent storm. Over the course of a few days, underlying dysfunction and relational issues bubble to the surface and eventually come to an uncontrollable roiling boil. It takes a certain level of genius to pull off a story that takes place in a bathroom. No. Scene. Changes.

That's a resignation of almost everything a writer would lean on to drive the story. Everything except the characters performing under laser point focus. To be honest, it's uncomfortable for the reader. I felt a claustrophobic tension for damn near the entirety of this novella, a low-level threat to your emotions as you watch a family wind up to a startling, disturbing finish.

Did I enjoy it? I mean, enjoyment is the wrong word. I can't say I took pleasure in experiencing everything Max put these characters through—I was especially invested in one of them, and I knew about halfway through there would be some sacrifice, pain, and suffering. So, enjoyment is the wrong word.

I endured it. I respect it. And it further cemented in my mind that Max Booth III is one of the most talented horror writers working in the industry right now. *We Need To Do Something* testifies.

AT A GLANCE

THEMES: Witchcraft, family drama/dysfunction, death, storms, survival, trapped, problem solving, infidelity, verbal abuse, overbearing fathers, teens

TONE: Bleak, Brutal, Disorienting, Disturbing, Intensifying Dread, Shocking, Violent

STYLE: Brisk Pacing, Character-Driven, Multiple POV

SETTING: Bathroom

PUBLISHER: Indie/Perpetual Motion Machine

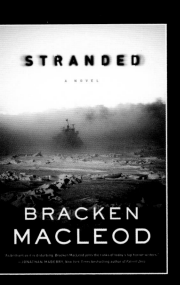

STRANDED

BY BRACKEN MACLEOD (2016)

"This is a bad idea," Connor said. Noah nodded in agreement. "There are no good ideas left."

AT A GLANCE

THEMES: Cargo ships, sailors, storm at sea, contagious Illness, disoriented, fog, stranded, trust

TONE: Eerie, Intensifying Dread, Menacing, Suspenseful

STYLE: Brisk Pacing, Character-Driven, Cinematic, Intricately Plotted

SETTING: Somewhere in the Arctic

PUBLISHER: Traditional/Tor Books

I'm not an adventurous person in real life, so I love reading stories about high-risk excursions. Through powerful descriptive language, I felt like I was right there, navigating through a dangerous, icy Arctic Sea. This horror story even hit on my affinity for "horror with heart." This is a must-have for any fan of quality, character-driven, suspenseful horror.

Our protagonist, Noah Cabot, is an interesting guy. I relished in his flashbacks, which created a complicated, unlikely hero I fell in love with. I felt like the crew he works with, including his father-in-law, on the *Arctic Promise* don't know him the way the reader gets to know him. MacLeod builds complicated relationships between the crew members, creating a tension that is already tight as the crew heads into disaster.

As the men of the *Arctic Promise* are tested under stress, MacLeod expertly begins to weave in the supernatural horror and starts dropping these "cliffhanger" moments at the end of every chapter. I'm such a cliffhanger addict, I knew at around 150 pages that I was going to be finishing this book over one weekend.

The pacing is perfect. I can tell that outlining and plot planning is MacLeod's wheelhouse because I felt that every piece of this story was placed with very precise intentionality. Highly recommend saving this one for winter months.

THE DEEP

BY NICK CUTTER (2015)

This darkness was ageless. And it had been
waiting a long time for Luke to inherit it.

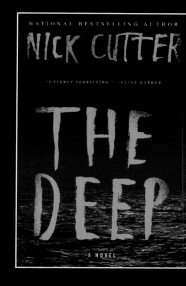

This is from my Goodreads update at 75 percent finished: "Last bit of
this book will be finished tonight with a full review tomorrow. SO
SCARY. I have been very horrified, disturbed, repulsed, claustrophobic—everything. The whole range of icky feelings. LOVE IT. Can't
wait to see how this ends."

The Deep was nominated for a Goodreads Choice Award in 2015, and
Stephen King had this to say about it: "scared the hell out of me and I
couldn't put it down . . . old-school horror at its best."

These quotes are here to serve as a warning. Every Nick Cutter horror
novel is an opportunity for optimum terror.

The Deep features a global pandemic that is threatening human civilization at a rapid rate. Luke goes to check in on his brother, who is
part of a small team of scientists studying an organic substance at the
bottom of the Mariana Trench. Cutter immerses the reader in Luke's
journey to the undersea lab. It's wildly uncomfortable, especially
if you suffer from particular fears or phobias like claustrophobia
(closed-in spaces or suffocation) or thalassophobia (fear of the ocean,
deep water, drowning). When he arrives at the undersea lab, he is
immediately concerned about the mental health of the crew due to
some . . . unusual discoveries.

There is nothing to prepare you for the unfathomable horror of this
book. Nick Cutter is the master of graphic, detailed descriptions of
the most god-awful atrocities. His speciality is insects, so whenever
his characters run across something to do with insects, it's always
very, very gross. There's plenty of nasty body horror, cosmic terror,
and just this overarching sense of isolation and dread. Your brain is
constantly on high alert with the feeling that "something is not right
here," and it's true. Nothing that happens in this book is "right."

AT A GLANCE

THEMES: Pandemic, scientific
research, brothers, deep sea,
hallucinations, isolation, close
quarters, rescue mission

TONE: Blood-Soaked,
Disturbing, Intensifying Dread,
Shocking, Violent

STYLE: Brisk Pacing,
Character-Driven, Cinematic,
Intricately Plotted, Stephen
King(ish)

SETTING: Pacific Ocean

PUBLISHER: Traditional/
Gallery Books

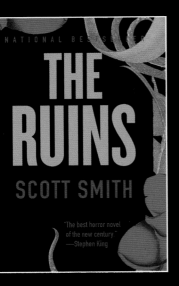

"The best horror novel of the new century."
—Stephen King

THE RUINS

BY SCOTT SMITH (2006)

Stacy wasn't certain; she'd never bothered to pay attention to details like that, and was always regretting it, the half knowing, which felt worse than not knowing at all, the constant sense that she had things partly right, but not right enough to make a difference.

I recommend this book so much, and I always tell people it's about a bunch of assholes on vacation who make a bunch of bad decisions that ultimately lead to a life-and-death situation. I didn't care about any of the characters. The book is well-written and compelling, and it's incredibly easy to settle into the pace and fly through the pages. No emotional investment necessary.

Two college-age couples are in Cancún, Mexico, drinking and partying with other guests at their hotel. One of their new acquaintances is worried about his brother who left for an archeological expedition to the Mayan Ruins and hasn't returned. He has a simple, hand-drawn map and is seeking help. The two couples stupidly decide to join the search with minimal preparations and little to no knowledge in their brains. They bring tons of alcohol but not enough water or food to keep anyone alive for a few days.

This story is written in one continuous narrative with the points of view shifting between the characters without chapter breaks. Everything unfolds rather quickly. The author provides a minute-by-minute account of events as they happen. Every bad decision and every overlooked opportunity to turn things around is recorded for the reader to observe like an inevitable trainwreck. It's supremely entertaining and horrifying.

AT A GLANCE

THEMES: Vacations, missing person, survival, tourists, jungle, hostile nature

TONE: Atmospheric, Bleak, Intensifying Dread, Suspenseful, Violent

STYLE: Cinematic, Multiple POV

SETTING: Cancún, Mexico

PUBLISHER: Traditional/Alfred A. Knopf

ANNIHILATION

BY JEFF VANDERMEER (2014)

That's how the madness of the world tries to colonize you: from the outside in, forcing you to live in its reality.

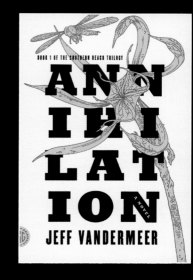

Area X. Probably the most terrifying geographical location in horror. Even the name of it strikes a certain level of fear into my heart. *Annihilation* is the story of the twelfth all-women expedition to venture beyond its quarantined borders. The eleven expeditions before this newest one have all ended in catastrophe.

The strongest aspect of horror in this book is that it's so disorienting. There are no character names, not even for the narrator. So, the reading experience resembles a "gathering of information" of our own; it feels like our own expedition into Area X.

Usually when there's a story about a team of people going on a mission, they all know and trust each other. The group of women going into Area X have not bonded into some sisterhood. They don't even trust each other. This level of isolation and caution between the characters is unsettling as they are forced to traverse alien territory as a unit. *Annihilation* is a master class in building dread through layers of unease and tension. The pacing is perfect.

VanderMeer's love for nature and his fascination with flora and fauna are utilized so well in the descriptions of the eerie setting and what the team members are encountering in their explorations. As a reader who is primarily out of my element adventuring outdoors, *Annihilation* taps into all my deepest fears about getting lost in an adverse, dangerous environment.

AT A GLANCE

THEMES: Psychological, scientific research, expeditions, missing persons, ambiguous government agency, women, sci-fi

TONE: Atmospheric, Eerie, Intensifying Dread, Suspenseful

STYLE: First-Person POV

SETTING: Somewhere on the coast

PUBLISHER: Traditional/ Farrar, Straus and Giroux

From Out of the Dark Came Blackness

BY RJ JOSEPH

Harboring an invisible heart full of darkness with nowhere to shelter and nurture it is a supremely lonely thing.

Whispers from beyond beckon you, begging indulgence in their decadent terrors. Fantastical obscurity becomes realty, curated to repel, yet fails to prompt escape. You remain in its presence because you are a creature of the night. Horror is you and you are it; your existence has been defined within the parameters of this beloved genre. The refuge it creates for your dark heart is perfection—almost.

You yearn, create, and imbibe every dark offering you can devour; scared, excited—wistful. Wearing the worlds like a skin. You indulge in wordplay, unsettlement, thriving in the stoked fears, even as more intimate fears are borne through. You long for the day you'll be included as more than just a spectator wearing a costume, temporary. Transient.

Hoping it comes . . . it must come.

You embark on a quest to find stories like yours, creators with whom you have a deeper kinship. *You can't be alone.* Understanding the existing stories are yours, yet not. You spiral across others who yearn for closeness, also wishing to speak through an enactment of the horrific worlds inside your minds. You long to meet, within the spaces between the words, to acknowledge you all are where you're destined to be: together in the darkness.

Years birth decades and gray hairs sprout more prolifically than opportunities, glinting, reflecting joys missed, stories untold through the restraint of invisibility. Compelled to create, you write yourself into existence in spaces where you don't have a reflection, a footprint—a beingness. Melting away when your efforts are snubbed, erasing you as if you were never even there.

It must come.

Contorting your words, education, and experiences to make them more palatable, more visible through a blanching of untruths that sever your tenuous grip on your own existence. Counterfeit scribblings, remotely true to human experiences but awash in the banality that prevails throughout the horror genre, assure you your erasure is the certain path to belonging. This fabricated journey circumnavigates your true direction, oppressing you with despondency as you lose hope of ever just *being* within the poignant darkness.

Eagerness turns to resentment turns to despair.

The domain of horror expands. The boundaries inhale the allowed narratives and can only exhale the same. Monotony permeates, inhibiting a flexible frame. Stagnant, brittle, it weeps for transformation, desiring to prevail—unable to do so without viable sustenance. The realm ruptures, shattering into miniscule fractions, creating fissures in the structure.

Fragments of the void wrap themselves around your essence and disperse your being throughout time. You are made alive through small deaths of immersion. Perfecting, learning, failing. Repeating. Your tenacity is not bravery; it is survival. Out of the dark, miniscule light shines through, highlighting, embellishing your Blackness. Never has minuteness felt so infinite, so brazen, so luminescent.

You move toward it.

The small shards gather into slices, images of your everyday mundane, your experiences, larger than origins and expirations. Giddiness propels you within domains and creations, until other pinpricks of illumination join you. You share existences with some. Others welcome you, still, dancing in your words, embracing your truths. *Seeing you.* Your paths intersect, sameness and differences dispersing into a oneness of novelty— spawning varying, beauteous paths.

You are seen.

Your belonging transverses simply seeing others who look like you. There is supreme comfort in the commonplace, the matter-of-factness present in living. Horror springs from these happenings, the extraordinary from the ordinary. The removal of yet one more point of disbelief that you don't have to suspend leaves open space to hang your hopes and dreams of more legitimacy, more attention. Celebration of your stories and you.

You persevere . . . this is about more than just you.

You continue to build the path of less soul-searing corridors for creators behind you to travel, with less loss of confidence and self. Pioneering creators originated the route for you, bleeding their essence, writing their truths—laying their hopes down to be trod upon in search of greatness, even as they have been erased. You commit to help as you have been helped, in perpetuity.

You rejoice at harboring a visible, sheltered, and nurtured heart full of darkness, in a sense of belonging.

Closed paths release their binds, welcoming the fantastic Blackness that resides within you. Your spirit comingles with those of your dark siblings, ushering in hordes of experiences gone hitherto unheard and untold. The sameness of the dark scatters, coalescing into distinct, unique, and titillating stories, fated to link together within the shadows. All are welcome, invited to record lifespans into eternal darkness, where experiences are conjoined by an irrefutable devotion to the creation and chronicling of horrors within horror.

This is about more than just you. You are seen. You create. It must come. It has come—from out of the dark came Blackness.

RJ Joseph is an award-winning, Bram Stoker Award®–nominated, Texas-based academic and creative writer. She has had works published in various venues, including *The Streaming of Hill House: Essays on the Haunting Netflix Series* and the Halloween 2020 issue of *Southwest Review*. When she isn't writing, reading, or teaching, she can usually be found wrangling her huge blended family.

SHORT STORY COLLECTIONS

I THINK SHORT FICTION IS ONE of the best formats for horror. Don't get me wrong; there are plenty of horror novels that more than represent the genre, but I do love the way a shorter, tighter story can give readers that glorious tension all the way through in one fell swoop. There's unrelenting terror page after page until suddenly, the story is over and you finally exhale. It's the best feeling.

They also offer the perfect way to get a sampling of all the different writing styles and subgenres an author dabbles in. So, when that moment inevitably comes and you hear about a new author you just *have* to read but you're not ready to invest in a whole novel or maybe you're not sure which book to buy because they're all different subgenres—it's an easy decision; buy their collection instead!

The collections I selected cover a lot of horror genre territory. The best horror writers are chameleons and can skillfully write in multiple subgenres. However, most, if not all of them, do feature horrible, nasty people—human monsters—making a lasting impact on the lives around them. My favorite thing to do is to *not* read a collection cover to cover but have one going between novels. Finish a novel, pick up a short story collection and read one story as a palette cleanser, then get on with your next favorite horror read.

THE BEAUTIFUL THING THAT AWAITS US ALL

BY LAIRD BARRON (2013)

Fear is a second heartbeat, my following shadow.

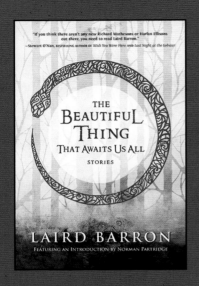

AT A GLANCE

THEMES: Cruelty in nature, the Pacific Northwest, criminals, the supernatural

TONE: Disturbing, Gruesome, Humorous, Intensifying Dread

STYLE: Cinematic, Intricately Plotted, Leisurely Paced

SETTING: Many are set in the Pacific Northwest

PUBLISHER: Indie/Night Shade

Holy Hell. There are some seriously terrifying tales in this collection. Each time I finished a story, I would think to myself, "Okay, that was probably the scariest one. The one I'll remember." And then the next one would top it!

First, there is "Hand of Glory," a story about this hired gun, this thug, who gets mixed up in some secret cabal of people who dabble in the dark arts. A hand is taken from a corpse and used as an evil talisman to keep the protagonist immobile. This was not the first time I've read about a Hand of Glory, so it was a real treat to revisit it here in an adult horror book. Later, there's talk of film or photographs being used to siphon people's souls while they engage with the media. A terrifying description of what's in the film gave me goosebumps.

"Vastation" is a monologue from some kind of superhuman being describing their existence over an endless period. I'm not sure exactly how the author intended this to land with readers, but I thought it was fascinating and hilarious at the same time, and it made my stomach feel weird thinking too much about time and space. It gave me an existential headache, but I loved it.

Lastly, one of the scariest short stories I've ever read is "The Men from Porlock." Some loggers go off into the woods on an errand and run across a tree with strange markings. As they try to make it back out the way they came, they discover a village of women that appear to be from another era. One of their own has been savagely murdered, and another man from the group is now missing. They're told he's locked in a tower. This whole situation goes from utterly horrific to mind-numbing terror in just a few pages.

The Beautiful Thing that Awaits Us All is one of the best collections of cosmic horror for readers to wrap their brains around. All of the stories work together as independent representations of cosmic horror tropes, such as secret cabals, cursed objects, ancient deities, and mind-melting "shakabuku"—a swift, spiritual kick to the head that alters your reality forever (thanks, *Grosse Pointe Blank*).

THINGS WE LOST IN THE FIRE

BY MARIANA ENRÍQUEZ (2016)

Yes, you're right, that house is an evil mask and it's not thieves behind it, there's a shuddering creature there. Something is hiding there that must not come out.

Reading through this collection was like a box of matches, okay? Hang with me here. Every time I started a story, it was like striking a match. A little whiff of sulfur dioxide, and then a flame . . . a hot burning flame that burns down the length of the wood until it burns the tips of your fingers. Ouch! It's a collection of Gothic, insidious, pitch-black dark tales set in modern Buenos Aires and teeming with danger.

The first story, "Dirty Kid," is about a woman obsessed with the life of a pregnant woman and her son who live on the street outside of her apartment. She's constantly mindful of the well-being of the son, the "dirty kid." Enríquez shows readers the underbelly of Buenos Aires—the hopelessness of drug addiction, children living in poverty, the constant threatening presence of narcos, and death. Death is everywhere. You have no idea where this story is going to go, but the overwhelming sense of dread is alarming; it won't be good.

There are haunted house stories, as well as tales with haunted people, drug addiction and other forms of self-destruction, murder, serial killers, unhealthy obsession, and a group of wild, reckless young women who hate everyone and everything.

Mariana Enríquez's unflinching, straightforward storytelling is addictive. Mesmerizing. Compulsive. *Things We Lost in the Fire* is one of the most provocative short story collections I've ever read.

AT A GLANCE

GRL PWR

THEMES: Poverty, drug addiction, drug cartel, violence, obsession, family, killers, superstitions

TONE: Disturbing, Gruesome, Intensifying Dread, Melancholy, Menacing, Shocking, Violent

STYLE: Cinematic, Critically Acclaimed

SETTING: Buenos Aires

PUBLISHER: Traditional/ Anagrama (Spanish); Hogarth Press (English translation, 2017)

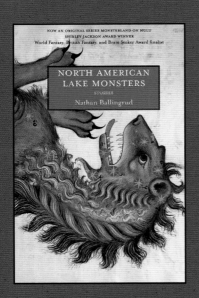

NORTH AMERICAN LAKE MONSTERS

BY NATHAN BALLINGRUD (2013)

She's like a thousand different people right now, all waiting to be, and every time she makes a choice, one of those people goes away forever. Until finally you run out of choices and you are whoever you are.

These are tales about what it means to be human with an emphasis on everyday life and our common struggles. There are human stories about humans, but also vampires, werewolves, and zombies. "Sunbleached" is a disquieting interaction that chilled me to the bone. Ballingrud's descriptions of the vampire's behaviors, movements, smell—it's all so alarming.

"You Go Where It Takes You" is the one that lingered the longest. It's brilliant in its simplicity; an examination of a single mother's desperation and how a perceptive stranger exploits it. I promise, you are unprepared for the emotional devastation that awaits you.

"The Way Station" is Ballingrud showing off one of his best assets, giving his readers eyes to see. In this story, we see New Orleans. Clearly, Ballingrud loves this city. Beltrane is a homeless man who is haunted by the ghost of New Orleans before Hurricane Katrina. It's a deeply emotional study of loss that can be applied to anyone suffering similar feelings.

The titular story is a painful examination of a father's integration back into the lives of his family after being incarcerated. There's an external mystery taking place outside of the family's home that intertwines with the internal turmoil of a family in transition after an emotional disruption and all the feelings that go along with that. It's beautiful and crushing at the same time with an exciting layer of immediate, urgent discovery threaded through it all.

This collection as a whole stands as a testament to Ballingrud's incredible contribution to horror. You know what to expect when you read his work: incredibly atmospheric and descriptive text, but never weighed down with unnecessary words. His prose is accessible, controlled, and concise, landing every intended punch.

AT A GLANCE

THEMES: Family, monsters, relationships, masculinity, desperation, supernatural

TONE: Atmospheric, Disturbing, Eerie, Gruesome

STYLE: Critically Acclaimed, Character-Driven, Intricately Plotted

SETTING: N/A

PUBLISHER: Indie/Small Beer Press

FALLING IN LOVE WITH HOMINIDS

BY NALO HOPKINSON (2015)

These are such human issues. I love and am fascinated by human beings. We are, all of us, capable of simultaneously such great good and such horrifying evil.

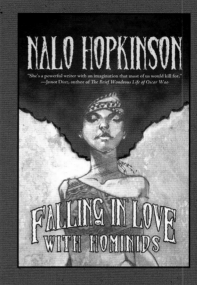

This collection won me over right out of the gate with the first story, "The Easthound." It starts with some young people out on the streets, hungry, looking for their next meal and trying to entertain themselves while also keeping one eye watching for the "sprouted"—people who have turned into werewolf-like beasts. From there, it's critically-acclaimed magic, Afro-Caribbean spirituality, science fiction, dark fantasy . . . a buffet of styles, genres, and tones. The one thing consistent throughout all the stories is the characters. They're so vibrant and alive.

In the story "Message in a Bottle," a man is quite content with the life he's made for himself. After babysitting his friend's daughter one day and getting drawn into this unusual child's life more than he wants to be, he says something that made me laugh out loud. I loved this protagonist after only spending several pages with him.

There's a story about a young girl struggling with body positivity and finding strength and power in a moment when she needs to save herself.

A mall filled with ghosts. An elephant breaking into a house. You'll even find a story that Peter Straub commissioned Nalo Hopkinson to write.

Some of these tales are micro-fiction, proving horror can be any length as long as it packs a punch. Take "Blushing," for example. A newlywed couple enters their new home for the first time together. The husband tells his wife not to enter the room he keeps locked. He soon discovers he doesn't need to keep secrets from his wife. Hopkinson is a true master at her craft, knowing exactly when to release that tension.

AT A GLANCE

GRL PWR

THEMES: Folklore, survival, family, gender, race, racism, identity, mythology, ghosts

TONE: Atmospheric, Dark, Eerie, Suspenseful

STYLE: Character-Driven, Cinematic, Critically Acclaimed, Lyrical

SETTING: N/A

PUBLISHER: Traditional/ Tachyon Publications

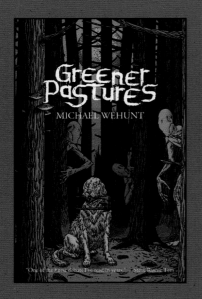

GREENER PASTURES

BY MICHAEL WEHUNT (2016)

These tales will get in your head and change you in ways you won't expect. That's what Wehunt does. Nothing you can do now but give in and accept the consequences.

Simon Strantzas, introduction of *Greener Pastures*

AT A GLANCE

THEMES: Grief, loss, loneliness, humanity, human nature, hope, pain, trauma

TONE: Eerie, Intensifying Dread, Melancholy, Menacing, Unsettling

STYLE: Abstract, Critically Acclaimed, Lyrical

SETTING: N/A

PUBLISHER: Indie/Shock Totem Publications; Apex Book Company (2017)

Reading *Greener Pastures* as a fledgling fan of indie horror was a life-altering experience. Not an exaggeration. My only frame of reference prior to this in terms of short story collections was that of the Stephen King variety. So this collection legitimately opened up the door to a whole new world of indie author collections.

Greener Pastures collects a variety of tales, unique in their own curious way but still resembling one another. The overall atmosphere while reading is eerie and disquieting as you tread through the landscape of these stories with trepidation. Most of the time, you will have no trouble finding familiar footing in which to stand, but occasionally, the path veers off into strange territories. These are my favorite parts: the weird and unusual.

A constant theme is loss, coupled with despair and loneliness. A very grim tone carries throughout the collection. However, once you've settled into these dark feelings, the opportunity to experience fear is right at the surface the entire time. It was a blooming sense of dread that I enjoyed.

An unnerving story that got right under my skin, "Greener Pastures" is one of the highlights of the collection. It transitions right into "A Discreet Music," a tale about a widower that left me in tears.

This became a recognizable pattern. "October Film Haunt: Under the House" terrified me, and then on its heels was "Deducted from Your Share in Paradise" bringing me to tears again. Pain, horror, sadness, pain, horror, sadness . . . wash, rinse, repeat. I loved every minute of this emotional wreckage.

THE GHOST SEQUENCES

BY A. C. WISE (2021)

*There's a reason we want to believe in ghosts.
We need them.*

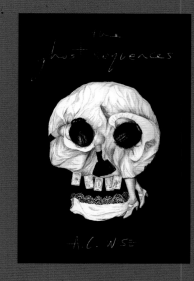

All I want is for A. C. Wise to tell me scary, haunting stories before I go to sleep. I think that's an impossible request, so I will settle for her published short stories in lieu of her physically being by my bedside every night.

I don't know how to impress upon you what an absolute gem of a book this is, but I will surely try. I will tell you about three stories that will hopefully entice and seduce you enough to smash that "Buy Now" button. But all of the stories here are worth the price of admission.

"How the Trick is Done" is a tale about a charming, charismatic magician capable of luring people to himself in a wildly self-serving, narcissistic way. The prose is luscious; the narrative is vulnerable and tragic. This haunting story explores how psychologically damaging love can be in the hands of a sociopath.

"The Stories We Tell About Ghosts" is hands down one of my all-time favorite short stories. With child protagonists, this whole "found-media" vibe, and ghosts, it's fucking scary. Some kids are using an app on their phones like Pokémon Go, except instead of finding cartoony Pokémon, they're collecting ghosts. You must experience this one for yourself. This is what a good ghost story feels like—utterly terrifying.

"The Last Sailing of the 'Henry Charles Morgan' in Six Pieces of Scrimshaw" comes with a warning: It's a mind-blower. This is one of the most original stories I've ever read. Another "found-media" vibe, the tale features a narrator who is describing artwork depicting the fate of a ship at sea and its crew. A strange creature depicted in the artwork is shown in various stages of an event that ultimately leads to a startling conclusion.

If you haven't found your groove with short stories, this could be the collection that unlocks it for you. A brilliant collection, cover to cover.

AT A GLANCE

THEMES: Trauma, grief, memory, death, ghosts, loss, magic, monsters, desire, obsession

TONE: Atmospheric, Eerie, Intensifying Dread, Menacing, Suspenseful

STYLE: Character-Driven, Cinematic, Critically Acclaimed, Intricately Plotted

SETTING: N/A

PUBLISHER: Indie/Undertow Publications

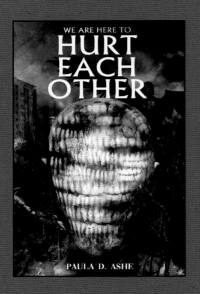

WE ARE HERE TO HURT EACH OTHER

BY PAULA D. ASHE (2022)

He held my hand as the chemical ate away at my mask, leaving the bone and muscle somewhat damaged but relatively intact.

I am a blistered, blasted nightmare.

What, underneath, are you?

AT A GLANCE

THEMES: Urban decay, desperation, depravity, addiction, loss, despair, hopelessness, killers

TONE: Bleak, Blood-Soaked, Brutal, Disturbing, Gruesome, Violent

STYLE: Brisk Pacing, Cinematic, Clive Barker(ish), Intricately Plotted

SETTING: N/A

PUBLISHER: Indie/Self-Published

This short story collection is pure, unadulterated horror. The author, Paula D. Ashe, is not messing around. The first two tales follow a man with severe facial deformities stalking people—men, women, children, it doesn't matter—and using the power of suggestion to guide them into mutilating their faces. Sometimes worse things happen. Nightmare fuel.

The third story, "All the Hellish Cruelties of Heaven," will excite Clive Barker fans. Paula D. Ashe has a full mastery of language, using it to plumb the depths of utter darkness. She introduces readers to a religious cult that practices the Gospel of Suffering. These people prey on vagrants and outcasts, the invisible people of the streets, to make "converts" out of them through despicable methods of pain. This tale is utterly horrifying but compelling at the same time. You can't look away.

One of my favorite aspects of this collection is how the stories are so different in style and substance but also interconnected. It's like a dark thread woven through the whole book. There are awful, horrible people in this collection. I found nothing relatable, only cruelty after brutal cruelty, but Paula D. Ashe's prose is so lavish, so provocative, I can't help but sing this book's praises. Just don't fault me for the depravity inside.

I honestly can't recommend *We Are Here to Hurt Each Other* enough. Immediately upon finishing, I sought more of this author's work out. Reader beware.

SHIVER

BY JUNJI ITO (2015)

". . . a collection of unpleasant things . . ."

Junji Ito, from his author's notes on "Greased"

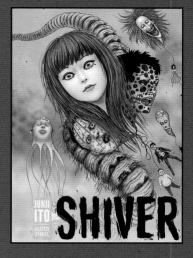

This. Is. Wild.

I honestly don't know how I lived my horror-loving life before Junji Ito. These stories tap fears I didn't even know I had. Grease? Acne? People's heads turning into balloons and chasing down their human counterparts so they can loop a noose around their necks and hang them? An unusually tall fashion model with a terrifying secret? Holes. Holes. HOLES!

I was already afraid of holes, I have trypophobia, but the story in this collection elevated it to a different plane of existence.

Japanese horror stories are wickedly unique. There's absolutely nothing available on the Western market even remotely this scary. I can confidently assure readers that if you're looking for a new horror experience or for something in between books to kickstart your nightmares, Junji Ito's imagination is a freaky place to spend some quality time. The illustrations range from disturbing to downright disgusting, repulsive, and vomit-inducing. I love it all! Pro tip: Look up a tutorial on how to read the panels in the right order if you haven't read manga before.

Want More Horror with Illustrations?

SLEWFOOT BY BROM

CRUEL WORKS OF NATURE: 11 ILLUSTRATED HORROR NOVELLAS BY GEMMA AMOR

CORALINE BY NEIL GAIMAN

THE DARK TOWER SERIES BY STEPHEN KING

THROUGH THE WOODS BY EMILY CARROLL

SCARY STORIES TO TELL IN THE DARK VOL. 1-3 BY ALVIN SCHWARTZ

THE THIEF OF ALWAYS: A FABLE BY CLIVE BARKER

THE HALLOWEEN TREE BY RAY BRADBURY

AT A GLANCE

THEMES: Vanity, cursed objects, fame, family, strange phenomena, ghosts, suicide, death

TONE: Brutal, Disturbing, Eerie, Gruesome, Shocking, Violent

STYLE: Cinematic

SETTING: N/A

PUBLISHER: Traditional/ VIZ Media LLC (English translation, 2017)

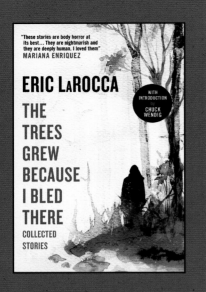

> "These stories are body horror at its best... They are nightmarish and they are deeply human. I loved them"
> MARIANA ENRIQUEZ

ERIC LaROCCA

THE TREES GREW BECAUSE I BLED THERE

COLLECTED STORIES

WITH INTRODUCTION CHUCK WENDIG

THE TREES GREW BECAUSE I BLED THERE

BY ERIC LAROCCA (2023)

I imagine my arms hardening into branches, my hair exploding with tiny emerald buds until I'm a beloved secret tucked away in some distant field—a birthplace for small birds and insects, a hallowed sanctuary for the weak and afflicted.

AT A GLANCE

THEMES: Tragedy, trauma, relationships, queer experience, love, obsession, human depravity, family, taboo

TONE: Atmospheric, Bleak, Brutal, Disturbing, Intensifying Dread, Melancholy, Shocking

STYLE: Character-Driven, Clive Barker(ish), Vignettes

SETTING: N/A

PUBLISHER: Traditional/Titan Books

It took forever to decide which LaRocca book to feature. Ultimately, I felt this collection would be the best possible introduction to everything Eric LaRocca has to offer. What's fascinating about LaRocca's storytelling is his ability to draw on specificity as he plumbs the depths of human emotions. You can expect the unexpected but not just for the sake of being strange. Expect these stories to probe, pierce, or puncture any barriers or protective layers in place.

In the story "Bodies are for Burning," the main character struggles with intrusive thoughts. LaRocca exposes the reality of a mental health crisis, and it's hard to be in that intimate shared space with someone who is imagining horrific scenarios while in the company of their infant niece. This one lingers.

"The Trees Grew Because I Bled There" is an unsettling imbalance of reciprocity in a relationship. Givers and takers. I loved the escalating tension of the story and the way it pairs with the tone of the narrator. Exquisite.

"You're Not Supposed to Be Here" was my first real encounter with LaRocca's work. A married couple is enjoying a day outdoors at a park with their small child. Their day is interrupted by an odd stranger. Done. That's all you need to know.

Lastly, I wanted to talk about "Please Leave or I'm Going to Hurt You." This is one of those stories that will live rent-free in your brain for the rest of your life because of the nature of this love story. In just a few pages, LaRocca brilliantly and effortlessly develops complex, multifaceted, incestual romantic feelings of a son for his father. It's as heartbreaking as it is disturbing, and readers will be helpless against LaRocca's magnetic pull no matter how much you don't want to know the story. Mesmerizing. I read it twice.

TRIBAL SCREAMS

BY OWL GOINGBACK (2018)

"You claim to be the world's greatest alligator wrestler,"
Wowakan continued, "but that is not true, either. Is
it? You may fool the tourists, but you didn't fool me.
The gator you wrestled tonight was blind." Harry was
shocked. "How did you know that?" "He told me,"
Wowakan replied.

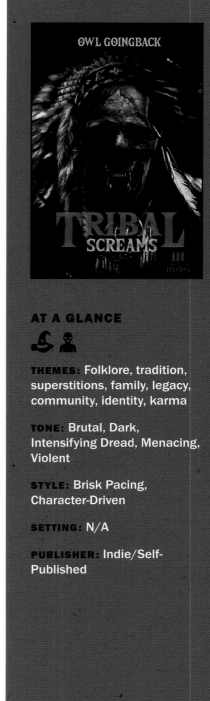

I bet I can sell you on reading this collection just by telling you that
Owl Goingback has worked as a cemetery caretaker and a paranormal
investigator. Who doesn't want to hear tales of horror from someone with that kind of life experience? Not only that but Goingback
infuses his stories with his Choctaw and Cherokee heritage. *Tribal
Screams* is a collection of short fiction, myths, legends, and lessons.

Horror fans will find brutal tales of zombies, human monsters,
ghosts, and creatures. The first story, "Tacachale," is a cautionary tale
with a familiar life lesson: The evil you put out into the world will
come back to you. No matter how many ways this truth is told, it's
always satisfying when awful people get what they deserve.

Goingback's storytelling blends in elements of fantasy and folklore
to complement strong, emotional themes of basic human needs: love,
purpose, and belonging. Nominated for the Nebula Award, "Grass
Dancer" is a story about a young man, Roger Thunder Horse, who
is drafted to serve in the Vietnam War, leaving behind his brother,
Jimmy. Roger's role in their community needs to be filled, so Jimmy
takes his brother's place as a dancer during a pow wow even though
he is disabled. I can't tell you what ultimately happens, but the way
this story made me feel was worth the price of admission all by itself.
While that particular story showcased the destruction war has on
communities and families, other tales lean into more primal fears,
making *Tribal Screams* a solid collection of horror.

AT A GLANCE

THEMES: Folklore, tradition,
superstitions, family, legacy,
community, identity, karma

TONE: Brutal, Dark,
Intensifying Dread, Menacing,
Violent

STYLE: Brisk Pacing,
Character-Driven

SETTING: N/A

PUBLISHER: Indie/Self-
Published

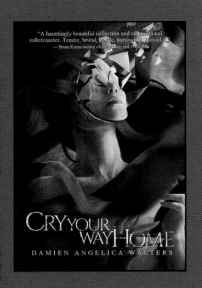

> "A hauntingly beautiful collection and an emotional rollercoaster. Tender, brutal, gentle, harrowing. I loved it."
> — Brian Keene author of *The Rising* and *Pressure*

CRY YOUR WAY HOME

BY DAMIEN ANGELICA WALTERS (2018)

Once upon a time there was a monster. This is how they tell you the story starts. This is a lie.

I have unrequited love for Damien Angelica Walters. *Cry Your Way Home* is one exceptional short story collection, and I just need her to know how much I want a huge section of my library filled up with her books. I have what's available, but it's not enough. It's not enough.

"Take A Walk in the Night My Love" is one of the greatest short stories I've ever read. This is, at first, about a married couple. Walters shows her audience the simple, habitual ways that people in long-term, committed relationships show love and care in even the most mundane situations. A woman wakes up and is startled by the discovery of dirt in the bed, on the sheets. She tells her husband. As the story moves on, you will begin to theorize as to what is happening between these two, but I promise you this: You have no idea. Just wait for it.

Another favorite story is "The Floating Girls: A Documentary." It reads like a transcript of a documentary following an unexplained phenomenon. Young women and girls, between the ages of eleven and seventeen, are floating up into the sky, never to be seen again. It's harrowing and haunting as it unflinchingly details the responses from those left behind.

Lastly, I'll point to "Tooth, Tongue, and Claw," a dark fairytale about a second-born daughter fated to be held captive by a beast. Per the tale itself, "This is not a love story. He will always be a monster, she will always wear a chain."

Damien Angelica Walters's stories are an essential fixture in the horror genre's landscape as clear indicators that the female experience is often marred by the horror of this world. Nobody can tell these tales better than women, and among these women, Damien Angelica Walters.

AT A GLANCE

THEMES: Marriage, the female experience, strange phenomena, love, relationships, deception, betrayal, trauma, sorrow, loss

TONE: Atmospheric, Dark, Disturbing, Eerie, Unsettling

STYLE: Character-Driven, Cinematic, Critically Acclaimed, Leisurely Paced

SETTING: N/A

PUBLISHER: Indie/Apex Book Company

SHE SAID DESTROY

BY NADIA BULKIN (2017)

The Goat came back—on the eve of jum—at kliwon, no less, spirit's night. She descended onto the house and draped her many wooly arms over the windows, blocking out the moon. Then she seeped through the roof and drenched the walls with wool-grease and the dirt of twenty cities, the blood of six hundred. The house has always been hers.

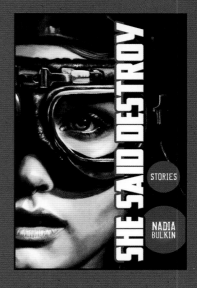

Quite like the way listening to every song on a favorite album builds into an overall mood, *She Said Destroy* is a collection of thirteen horror stories that collectively set a dark, haunting atmosphere for readers to immerse themselves in.

Upon closer inspection, Bulkin extends an invitation into a culture unlike your own. An experience you've never had before. A glimpse of a world you don't live in. The intimate feelings of someone you don't know going through a tragedy you'll never have to endure.

In my favorite story, "Red Goat, Black Goat," Kris arrives at an estate to start her new babysitting job and quickly learns that the children are already being watched—or rather, protected . . . maybe haunted—by the Goat Nurse. I read this story with my eyelids peeled back as far as they would go and I never blinked while I read. Although, I did flinch.

Horror readers are given a special gift by authors: teaching us how to broaden our capacity for empathy in the real world by braving other people's harsh realities through their fictional accounts. We live all these different lives when we slip inside a character so unlike us. This is the collection that taught me this truth.

As I came out of the mainstream book market and discovered independently published horror, I realized that all the voices I had been reading sounded the same. Bulkin's collection opened my eyes to storytelling that challenged my worldview; it gave me thought-provoking situations that I could mull over and chew on. The complexities and nuances lingered long after reading, and I hope that they will do the same for a wider audience.

AT A GLANCE

 GRL PWR

THEMES: Folklore, the female experience, socio-political, ghosts, family, tradition, identity, sexuality

TONE: Disorienting, Disturbing, Grim, Intensifying Dread, Melancholy, Shocking

STYLE: Character-Driven, Critically Acclaimed, Leisurely Paced, Lyrical

SETTING: N/A

PUBLISHER: Indie/Word Horde

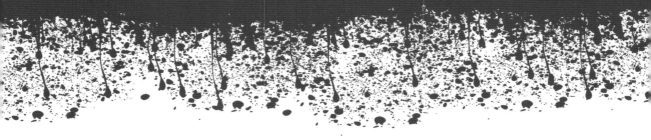

The Sharpest Stake

BY DANIEL KRAUS

Horror spikes roughly once per decade, and with all the energy of a Van Helsing doing in a Dracula. But even among those spikes there are *sharper* spikes: the Universal horror films of the 1930s–40s and the attendant IP; the 1980s goo-splosion of gore and the ascendance of Stephen King; and whatever it is we're living through right now—I suspect we won't know how to capsulize it until the next fallow period craters before us.

Why *now*? It's the question I get asked more than any other. Makes sense—it's the same question authors like me recreationally mull. Why *us*?

The stock answer goes something like this. Netflix's *Stranger Things* was a PG-13 hit welcoming all sorts of viewers; the show's King-y tone spurred a renaissance of King adaptations created by lifelong fans; the popular upswell midwifed star creators like Jordan Peele and Luca Guadagnino, top-tier artists *choosing* to work in horror instead of trying to fight their way out of it; and finally, there was the art/commerce doublet of smaller companies (like A24) harnessing the zeitgeist while larger ones churned out reboots for the presumed troglodytes who just wanted to see their favorite masks again.

You will, of course, notice an aggravating throughline to this argument: *all the examples are movies.* I know all too well that books, in a capitalistic sense, are the crumbs on the shoes of the movie and video-game industries, and often flow with the winds created by those more lucrative art forms. One of my most depressing refrains is that an atrocious movie adaptation will result in the best PR a book will ever get in its life. Very sad, very true.

But Stephen King bucked that trend in the 1980s. He was the driver, not production companies, and he's back at the wheel now. My senses tell me that, for the first time, a true bifurcation is developing between books and movies, which speaks loudly about how hard horror authors are pushing the gas pedal. This is due in large part to online connectivity. The granularity of taste that can be served today makes another Mr. King practically impossible to create. And that's a good thing! Instead of a single, roaring, 1958 Plymouth Fury dominating the horror road, we have a few thousand punks on skateboards—and as a result, the genre has never, ever, *ever* been richer.

So why the return of the sharp spike? There is, of course, the satisfying if simplistic historical calculus. WWI begat Universal horror; the Vietnam War era begat *Night of the Living Dead*; Reaganomics begat splatterpunk; Abu Ghraib begat torture porn. These theories, which likely contain traces of truth, are appealing because they make artistic hay out of events that otherwise feel like nothing but bleak harbingers of humanity's end.

My theory of what's happening today is less dramatic but even more overriding. As more of our interactions with fellow humans shift online, we are *feeling* less and less viscerally. Stakes are dulled through a virtual interface. How much quicker are people to say "I love you" or "You're an asshole" online as compared to IRL? We run a whole lot hotter via gadgets, but engines that never quit running have side effects. We become numb. Our emotions cauterize. We are, in fact, a little bit dead. Deader, I would argue, than we've ever been before.

Horror brings those severed nerves back to screaming life.

Never have we so desperately needed to feel—simply *feel*. A global pandemic rife with quarantines, long periods of sheltering in place, and workplaces that have moved entirely online has violently exacerbated this need. Far more effective in raising us than any ancient curse, zombie virus, or vampiric blood strain is the jolting upset of

reading Agustina Bazterrica's novel, *Tender Is the Flesh*. The gut-deep revulsion/delight of each page turn of Ed Piskor's comic *Red Room*. The hopeless disorientation of Adam Poots's board game *Kingdom Death: Monster*. The discomfiting duality of Keiichiro Toyama's video game *Siren* putting you in the monster's eyes.

Horror has always been catharsis. Most genres are, in one way or another. Now, as we stagger into a future of VR avatars and AI "art," horror is transmuting into something even more vital: life itself. A connection to our flesh-and-blood reality. A reminder to respond to the world that is actually around us, not merely the representations of it. A call to value the people, the real ones, that are out there, just beyond our screens. If it takes hideously upsetting events at the hands of artists like Victor LaValle or Tananarive Due or Gretchen Felker-Martin to make us care again, so be it.

The sharpest spike has returned—and I wonder if it might be planted so deeply this time that it can never be whittled away again.

Daniel Kraus is the *New York Times*-bestselling author of 20 books, including *The Shape of Water* and *Trollhunters* (with Guillermo del Toro), *The Living Dead* (with George A. Romero), and *The Death and Life of Zebulon Finch*, one of *Entertainment Weekly*'s Top 10 Books of the Year. He is a multiple Bram Stoker Award finalist.

You're a Horror Junkie! Now What?

Eat all the candy you can, until it makes you sick.
And then eat some more.

— Stephen Graham Jones, *The Least of My Scars*

So, listen, I hate to tell you this, but reading a steady diet of horror is going to ruin you for other genres. You'll be reading some fantasy novel, and you're going to start thinking things like:

When is this going to get nasty?

I wish one of the characters would just get murdered already.

I hope the landscape goes on a violent, bloody rampage.

Maybe this beautiful cottage is haunted by a vengeful spirit!

Unfortunately, nothing will satisfy these needs quite like horror. Let me just make sure you know how to get that sweet, sweet hook-up 24/7.

Demain Publishing: Short, Sharp, Shocks! Trust me, you need these in your life. If you have an e-Reader, you can fill it up with quality, short, deliciously evil stories written by modern, indie horror authors for the price of coffee in a 1950s diner. I have read at least twenty of them and they're all excellent. I love this series.

Horror Anthologies: You need to start reading anthologies. I have found so many new-to-me authors after enjoying their stories in a themed anthology. I recommend anything edited by Ellen Datlow first and foremost. She is a legendary anthologist, curating the absolute best of the best when it comes to horror. She releases a *Best of Horror* volume every year. Some of my favorite themed collections are: *Echoes* (ghost stories), *Final Cuts* (Hollywood Horror), *Body Shocks* (extreme body horror), *When Things Get Dark* (Shirley Jackson-inspired), and *Edited By* (a tribute to Ellen Datlow herself). Christopher Golden has some amazing anthologies too, including one that I read every year at Christmas called *Hark the Herald Angels Scream* (Christmas Horror) and *Hex*, which he co-edited with Kelly Armstrong (All women, all witch tales). Also, *Human Monsters*, the anthology I edited with my business partner Ashley Saywers, is a feast of new talent, seasoned horror veterans, and rising stars.

PseudoPod: Here's a horror fiction podcast dedicated to showcasing short fiction in audio format. I have found so many new favorites by listening to stories by authors that are totally new to me. I haven't heard one yet that hasn't wowed me. This is where I discovered Wendy Wagner (*The Deer Kings*) and went on to buy two signed books for my collection, as well as A.C. Wise (*The Ghost Sequences*).

Horror Magazines: So many of the short story collections I included on my list feature stories that were originally published in anthologies or magazines. I recommend buying one issue of a magazine before you decide to subscribe. I can recommend the ones I have read and enjoyed, but there are so many out there. Shop around to find the ones you like the best.

- *Dark Matter Magazine* is a print and digital publication of dark sci-fi and horror stories, artwork, author interviews, and other features. Every issue includes at least eight original stories, one reprint story, two art features, an author interview, and dozens of color illustrations for anywhere between 130 to 180 pages of content.

- *Apex Magazine* is an online zine of dark fiction, interviews, essays, and a monthly podcast.

- *Nightmare Magazine* features horror and dark fantasy, typically a mix of reprints and originals edited by author/editor Wendy Wagner. It also includes other features like interviews, book reviews, Q & A, and non-fiction articles.

Follow Me on Twitter and Instagram: Look up "Mother Horror"/Sadie Hartmann. I curate my social media platform to promote everything horror fiction has to offer. I do huge round-ups of book recommendations by tropes, subgenres, and themes. I promote new releases and review what I'm currently reading. There are tons of horror influencers on Instagram, and I typically share their content in my stories so you can find them easily.

Night Worms: Here's my shameless plug for my horror fiction subscription service I curate monthly with my business partner Ashley. You can have the latest and greatest horror fiction, chosen by two obsessive fangirls, delivered monthly to your door with some extra goodies like coffee, bookmarks, stickers, signed bookplates, and more. Check us out online! We are a boutique service with limited availability, so keep an eye on our social media to learn when we are open for exclusive subscription opportunities.

Bram Stoker Award Reading Lists, Nominated Work, and Winners: Keep your finger on the pulse of what the HWA (Horror Writers Association) is doing, and make sure to check out award-winning work. The ceremonies happen every year, and they're a great resource for finding quality horror.

The Shirley Jackson Awards, Nominated Works, and Winners: This is a juried, annual awards ceremony for "outstanding achievement in the literature of psychological suspense, horror, and the dark fantastic."

Emily Hughes' Annual "Horror We're Looking Forward To" List: This is a free service that Emily Hughes compiles every year and it is an invaluable resource. It used to be a feature of the Tor Nightfire blog but now Emily is posting it on her own platform, ReadJumpScares.com. I literally look at it at least once a week to curate my reading lists and organize my incoming review books by date according to this list. Bookmark it on your browser and check it every month to see what's new.

Newsletters: Sign up for your favorite author's newsletters and get updates directly from the source.

Follow Stephen King on Twitter: Keeping tabs on Stephen King on Twitter gives you a chance to make note of his recommendations. I have found several favorite books based on his endorsements.

NoveList Plus: This database is available through your public library. First off, the library is an incredible resource. With free audiobooks, books, special orders and requests, and interlibrary borrowing, essentially you can get every book you want for free if you're willing to wait a little bit for popular titles. The perk to NoveList is that it's a database of books curated by librarians powered by a strong search engine that can filter and sort titles based on a whole host of keyword searches. When you search for a book, it will provide a synopsis, read-alike recommendations, librarian reviews, and other critical reviews. My "At a Glance" section of every recommendation in this book is heavily influenced by my time spent researching these books on NoveList. I use it almost every day.

Book Checklist

ALPHABETIZED BY BOOK TITLE

1. ☐ *A Lush and Seething Hell* by John Hornor Jacobs

2. ☐ *A Place for Sinners* by Aaron Dries

3. ☐ *The Ancestor* by Danielle Trussoni

4. ☐ *Annihilation* by Jeff VanderMeer

5. ☐ *Baby Teeth* by Zoje Stage

6. ☐ *The Ballad of Black Tom* by Victor LaValle

7. ☐ *The Beautiful Thing That Awaits Us All* by Laird Barron

8. ☐ *Beneath* by Kristi DeMeester

9. ☐ *The Bone Weaver's Orchard* by Sarah Read

10. ☐ *The Book of Accidents* by Chuck Wendig

11. ☐ *The Bottoms* by Joe R. Lansdale

12. ☐ *Boys in the Valley* by Philip Fracassi

13. ☐ *Broken Monsters* by Lauren Beukes

14. ☐ *Camp Slaughter* by Sergio Gomez

15. ☐ *Children of Chicago* by Cynthia Pelayo

16. ☐ *The Children on the Hill* by Jennifer McMahon

17. ☐ *Come Closer* by Sara Gran

18. ☐ *Coyote Songs* by Gabino Iglesias

19. ☐ *Cry Your Way Home* by Damien Anjelica Walters

20. ☐ *December Park* by Ronald Malfi

21. ☐ *The Deep* by Nick Cutter

22. ☐ *The Deer Kings* by Wendy Wagner

23. ☐ *The Demonologist* by Andrew Pyper

24. ☐ *Devil's Creek* by Todd Keisling

25. ☐ *Falling in Love with Hominids* by Nalo Hopkinson

26. ☐ *The Fearing* by John F. D. Taff

27. ☐ *The Fisherman* by John Langan

28. ☐ *Full Immersion* by Gemma Amor

29. ☐ *The Ghost Sequences* by A.C. Wise

30. ☐ *The Ghost Tree* by Christina Henry

31. ☐ *Ghoul* by Brian Keene

32. ☐ *Gone to See the River Man* by Kristopher Triana

33. ☐ *Good Neighbors* by Sarah Langan

34. ☐ *Goth* by Otsuichi

35. ☐ *Greener Pastures* by Michael Wehunt

36. ☐ *Grind Your Bones to Dust* by Nicholas Day

37. ☐ *The Grip of It* by Jac Jemc

38. ☐ *The Hacienda* by Isabel Cañas

39. ☐ *Heart-Shaped Box* by Joe Hill

40. ❐ *Hearts Strange and Dreadful* by Tim McGregor

41. ❐ *Hex* by Thomas Olde Heuvelt

42. ❐ *I'm Thinking of Ending Things* by Iain Reid

43. ❐ *In the Valley of the Sun* by Andy Davidson

44. ❐ *Just Like Home* by Sarah Gailey

45. ❐ *Kill Creek* by Scott Thomas

46. ❐ *Kin* by Kealan Patrick Burke

47. ❐ *Knock Knock* by S. P. Miskowski

48. ❐ *Last Days* by Brian Evenson

49. ❐ *The Last Days of Jack Sparks* by Jason Arnopp

50. ❐ *The Laws of the Skies* by Grégoire Courtois

51. ❐ *The Library at Mount Char* by Scott Hawkins

52. ❐ *The Listener* by Robert McCammon

53. ❐ *Little Eve* by Catriona Ward

54. ❐ *The Loop* by Jeremy Robert Johnson

55. ❐ *Mexican Gothic* by Silvia Moreno-Garcia

56. ❐ *The Nightmare Girl* by Jonathan Janz

57. ❐ *North American Lake Monsters* by Nathan Ballingrud

58. ❐ *Number One Fan* by Meg Elison

59. ❐ *Of Foster Homes and Flies* by Chad Lutzke

60. ❐ *PenPal* by Dathan Auerbach

61. ❐ *Red* by Jack Ketchum

62. ❐ *Red Hands* by Christopher Golden

63. ❐ *Red X* by David Demchuk

64. ❐ *The Return* by Rachel Harrison

65. ❐ *Revelator* by Daryl Gregory

66. ❐ *Ring Shout* by P. Djèlí Clark

67. ❐ *Rites of Extinction* by Matt Serafini

68. ❐ *The Ruins* by Scott Smith

69. ❐ *She Said Destroy* by Nadia Bulkin

70. ❐ *Shiver: Selected Stories* by Junji Ito

71. ❐ *The Silence* by Tim Lebbon

72. ❐ *Stranded* by Bracken MacLeod

73. ❐ *Suffer the Children* by Craig DiLouie

74. ❐ *The Switch House* by Tim Meyer

75. ❐ *Tender is the Flesh* by Augustina Bazterrica

76. ❐ *Things We Lost in the Fire* by Mariana Enríquez

77. ❐ *Transmuted* by Eve Harms

78. ❐ *The Trees Grew Because I Bled There* by Eric LaRocca

79. ❐ *Tribal Screams* by Owl Goingback

80. ❐ *True Crime* by Samantha Kolesnik

81. ❐ *The Twisted Ones* by T. Kingfisher

82. ❐ *Walk the Darkness Down* by John Boden

83. ❐ *We Are Here to Hurt Each Other* by Paula D. Ashe

84. ❐ *We Need to Do Something* by Max Booth III

85. ❐ *When the Reckoning Comes* by LaTanya McQueen

86. ❐ *White Horse* by Erika T. Wurth

87. ❐ *The Wicked* by James Newman

88. ❐ *The Wingspan of Severed Hands* by Joe Koch

89. ❐ *The Worm and His Kings* by Hailey Piper

90. ❐ *The Year of the Witching* by Alexis Henderson

91. ❐ *Zone One* by Colson Whitehead

AUTHOR SPOTLIGHTS

92. ❐ Adam Nevill

93. ❐ Alma Katsu

94. ❐ Ania Ahlborn

95. ❐ Christopher Buehlman

96. ❐ Grady Hendrix

97. ❐ Josh Malerman

98. ❐ Paul Tremblay

99. ❐ Stephen Graham Jones

100. ❐ Tananarive Due

101. ❐ V. Castro

Acknowledgments

OTHERWISE KNOWN AS A BUNCH OF PEOPLE I NEED TO THANK BEFORE I'M MURDERED

My parents: Mom for being my first and favorite Constant Buddy Reader. Dad for always being in my corner, Team Sadie, even when I sucked at basketball.

Stephen King, my Constant Storyteller.

My husband and best friend, Dan Hartmann, for literally everything (especially the built-in bookshelves). Ryan, Natalie, and Andrew Hartmann for all your love and encouragement. My sisters Emily & Sarah, I miss reading *Scary Stories to Tell in the Dark* to you. George and Mary Hartmann & Jen and Paul Legge: thank you for all your excitement and encouragement.

My editor, Alexandra Murphy at Page Street Publishing: Your love of the genre and belief in me manifested this whole thing into existence and I'll never get over it. The whole Page Street Team, including Sarah Monroe, Rosie Stewart, and Laura Benton. My publicist, Katelynn Jasper. The illustrator, Marco Fontanili, you brought everything to life!

My Night Worms business partner and bestie, Ashley Saywers, dream job unlocked! Mentors: Ellen Datlow, Brian Keene, and Becky Spratford. The entire #bookstagram community and all the buddy readers: Alex, Danni, Rayne, Tali, Marcy, Liz, Nina, Gina, Beth, Ally, Lori, The Horror Book Buying Maniacs, everyone!

All my editors over the years: Blu Gilliand (Cemetery Dance), Richard Cooper (*SCREAM* magazine), Joshua Chaplinsky (LitReactor), Lisa Quigley (The LineUp), Sam Boush (*Mystery & Suspense* magazine), Monica Kuebler (*Rue Morgue*), Angel Melanson (*Fangoria*), and Olaf Buchheim (Cemetery Dance Germany). The HWA.

Friends and Supporters: Danielle Trussoni, Janine Pipe, Cynthia Pelayo, Josh Malerman, Eric LaRocca, Izzy Lee, Paul Tremblay, Jeremy Robert Johnson, Jonathan Janz, Briana Morgan, Mark Steensland, Joe Sullivan, Richard Thomas, Joe Monti, Kasey & Joe R. Lansdale, Jonathan Levit, The Night Worms crew (Alex & Gillian).

Peg at Lahaska Bookshop. Destiny "howlinglibrary" for her insightful reviews and lists of trigger warnings, I took those into consideration multiple times. The Bookseller in Grass Valley, shoutout to the best hometown in the world. I love you, Grass Valley.

Long live horror,
Sadie Hartmann

About the Author

SADIE HARTMANN A.K.A. "MOTHER HORROR" is the co-owner of the horror fiction subscription company Night Worms, and the editor-in-chief of her own horror fiction imprint, Dark Hart. She had an award-winning Halloween costume in the seventh grade but was not invited to sit with the cool kids.

Born and raised in the small town of Grass Valley, CA, she now makes her home with her husband of 20+ years in the Pacific Northwest where they celebrate cloudy days, stare at Mt. Rainier, eat street tacos, and hang out with their three kids. They have a Frenchie named Owen.

Index